THE UNSEEN WORLD OF
Poppy Malone
A Gaggle of Goblins

SUZANNE HARPER

Greenwillow Books
An Imprint of HarperCollins*Publishers*

The Unseen World of Poppy Malone: A Gaggle of Goblins
Copyright © 2011 by Suzanne Harper

The text of this book is set in 12-point ITC Esprit.
Book design by Paul Zakris

Library of Congress Cataloging-in-Publication Data

Harper, Suzanne.
A gaggle of goblins / by Suzanne Harper.
p. cm. — (The unseen world of Poppy Malone)
"Greenwillow Books."
Summary: Nine-year-old Poppy's parents are paranormal investigators who have never actually found anything, but that may change when they move to Austin, Texas, and Poppy meets a goblin in the attic of their new house.
ISBN 978-0-06-199607-8 (trade bdg.)
[1. Goblins—Fiction. 2. Family life—Texas—Fiction.
3. Austin (Tex.)—Fiction.] I. Title.
PZ7.H23197Gag 2011   [Fic]—dc22   2010025558

11 12 13 14 15 LP/RRDB 10 9 8 7 6 5 4 3 2 1
First Edition

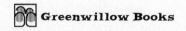
Greenwillow Books

For Bill Boedeker

Chapter
ONE

Poppy Malone wasn't the kind of girl who saw goblins. That was what made the whole thing so strange. If it had been anyone else in her family—her parents or Will or Franny or even Rolly, who was only five—it would have made much more sense.

But they didn't go into the attic on that hot June afternoon, and Poppy did. And that made all the difference.

"Why do we have to move all the time?" Poppy had complained in first grade when she, Will, and Franny were told they would have to change schools in the middle of the year. Not only would she have to start all over again at a brand-new school, but she would miss the big Halloween party at her old school, which she had been looking forward to for weeks. "Why can't we stay in one place like normal people?"

"Because your mother and I do not have normal jobs," Poppy's father had answered shortly. He had just finished reading the moving company's letter explaining how much they planned to charge, and he was in an irritable mood. "We go where the ghosts are."

Poppy's mother had put down her magnifying glass—she had been peering closely at a blurry photo of an alien spacecraft hovering over the White House—and beamed at her husband. "That's got a nice ring to it, Emerson," she had said. "It could be our new motto!" She repeated it more loudly, as if doing a voice-over for a TV commercial. "'We Go Where the Ghosts Are.'"

"And where the grants are, of course," Mr. Malone had added gloomily. "Not that there are many of those to chase these days! And even when we do land one, it barely covers our moving costs. Look at this bill, Lucille, and tell me exactly when out-and-out robbery was made legal in this country. . . ."

That had led to an extremely long and boring discussion about money and bills and not ordering so much takeout food, so Poppy had drifted away to brood over what her father had said. She realized, of course, that most of her friends did not have parents who tracked UFOs, pursued monsters, and investigated rumors of vampires. If she put her mind to it, she could even understand why some people might think her family's life was rather exciting. But that night, she had her dream for the first time, the dream that she would have dozens of times after that. In it, they were moving into yet another house, but this time the house felt mysteriously as if it were already her home, and her mother was saying, "Don't worry, Poppy, we're going to stay here for years and years and years." The dream always seemed so real that, for the longest time, she was sure it would come true.

Now, of course, she was much older—almost nine and three-quarters—and she knew the dream was simply the result of random discharges of neurons in her brain. If she needed any more evidence that dreams did not come true, Poppy only had to point to one fact: fourth grade had just ended and they were moving again. This time, Poppy's family was leaving Emporia, Kansas, where her parents had taught a ghost-hunting class at a local college for two semesters, and heading to Austin, Texas, where they had won a grant from a foundation interested in paranormal research.

This was Poppy's eighteenth move (she had started a journal to keep track), so she could predict exactly what would happen. She knew that Rolly would get spectacularly carsick before the first rest stop, that Franny would spend the entire trip sighing over some boy she'd left behind, and that Will would get a window seat. Once they got to their new house, they would spend days unpacking boxes, moving furniture around, and arguing over who got which bedroom. School would start, she would make a few friends, and then, before she knew it, they'd be moving again.

Everything, she thought drearily, would happen exactly as it always had before, her future would look exactly like her past, and there were no surprises in store for her at all. . . .

Then two days later, they arrived in Austin, Texas, drove down a tree-shaded street, and pulled into a long driveway.

"Well?" Mr. Malone said proudly. "What do you think of your new home?"

Everyone tumbled out of the car and stared at the three-story wooden house. The outside had once been painted purple, but had now faded to a soft lavender. A swing swayed lazily on the wide front porch; large, gnarled oaks cast a cool shade over the lawn; and a tortoiseshell cat slept on the front steps. The house looked worn and comfortable and exactly like the house in Poppy's dream.

She was too happy to say a word. She just stood there, smiling up at the house as the rest of her family headed for the front door.

And then everything had gone completely and utterly wrong.

"I sense something sinister here," Poppy's mother said two hours later. The movers hadn't yet delivered their furniture, but they had discovered two dusty chairs standing forlornly in the middle of a cavernous kitchen. Mrs. Malone was sitting on one with her foot propped up on the other, an ice pack tied onto her ankle. "Very sinister indeed."

She looked quite pleased at the idea.

"I'll tell you what's sinister," Mr. Malone grumbled as he tried to open one of the kitchen windows. "No air-conditioning, in the summer, in Texas!"

His wife gave him a sharp glance. "Perhaps you didn't hear me," she said stiffly. "I *said*—"

"And whoever decided to paint these windows shut was not just sinister," Mr. Malone interrupted, grunting as he shoved the window sash. "That person was diabolical."

"Speaking of diabolical," Mrs. Malone tried

again. "I was just saying that I feel that there is something malevolent in this house—"

"You're not pushing up at the right angle," Will told his father. Poppy's twin brother was sitting on the kitchen counter, drinking a soda. His brown hair was sticking up in damp spikes and his T-shirt was sweaty, but he still managed to look like a four-star general watching with disbelief as one of his soldiers botched an easy job. "You should bend your knees more. We studied this in science class. It's a simple problem of force and leverage—"

"Maybe you should try, then," his father suggested irritably. "After all, *I* only have a doctorate in applied physics. This problem is undoubtedly too simple for me to understand."

Unfazed, Will took another gulp of soda. "I'd be glad to demonstrate, but my shoulder still hurts."

Mrs. Malone spotted an opening and took it. "That is exactly what I was trying to tell you! There is Something Here that does not like us! The shoulder is simply the first bit of evidence. Consider!" She glanced around the kitchen, her blue eyes sparkling with delight. "First, the front door fell on Will and almost killed him."

If she had hoped to impress her audience, she was disappointed.

"Those hinges were ancient. They were practically crumbling with rust," Poppy said. She had brought their cooler in from the car, unloaded the last few snacks and sodas, and was now sitting on it and hoping that the movers would soon arrive with their furniture. "And, anyway, it was just a glancing blow."

"Serves Will right for trying to get inside before anyone else," Franny added. Her voice was somewhat indistinct, since she was washing her hair under the kitchen faucet, but she still managed to sound outraged. "It's so unfair! He always gets first dibs on the biggest bedroom, just because he's pushier than the rest of us."

Her mother ignored this. "Then Franny walked into the pantry and that sack of flour fell on her head—"

"That's not the same thing at all," Will

protested. "Flour's not dangerous. I probably won't make the football team now that my throwing arm's been hurt."

Franny flung back her head, spraying water over the kitchen. "I could have been suffocated," she pointed out, her long blond hair, usually so curly and golden, hanging down her back in sodden rat's tails. "I could have breathed that flour into my lungs and suffocated and *died*."

Poppy refrained from pointing out that Will's throwing arm was wildly inaccurate even before the door fell on him and that, as far as she knew, no one had ever been killed by a sack of flour.

Her mother refused to be diverted. "Then that venetian blind fell down, practically on poor little Rolly's head—"

"He probably pulled it down," Poppy said. "You know how he is."

Every head swiveled to look appraisingly at Rolly, who was prying up a linoleum tile with a fork.

Feeling the force of their stares, Rolly looked

up. "What?" he asked. Then before anyone could answer, he added, "I didn't do it."

"Of course you didn't, dear," his mother said warmly before returning to her main theme. "And then I tripped over that garden hoe." She gingerly wiggled her foot. "So unlike me."

Poppy did her best to inject a note of logic into the discussion. "Just because we've had a few accidents—"

"Accidents?" her mother asked. She raised one meaningful eyebrow. "Or evidence of unseen and possibly malevolent forces?"

"Accidents," Poppy said firmly. "There is a completely rational explanation for everything that's happened."

"Well, I'm certainly used to addressing the doubts of skeptics, although I didn't expect to be forced to do so within the bosom of my own family," said her mother. "Give me a moment to get in touch with my intuitive side." She took a deep, dramatic breath, then thrust her fingers through her dark curly hair and closed her eyes, humming nasally.

Poppy looked at her brother and crossed her eyes to show her mortification. Will just grinned back at her, kicking his feet and watching with interest as his mother went into a trance.

After a moment, Mrs. Malone's eyes opened. She stared soulfully into the distance. Then she said, in a deep, hollow voice, "There is a Dark Presence here."

This finally caught Mr. Malone's attention. He forgot the window and turned to stare at her, his eyes shining with excitement. "Really? That would be an amazing stroke of luck!" he said. "What do you think, Lucille? A poltergeist?"

"No, I don't think so," she said thoughtfully. "Their energy always has such a *spiteful* edge to it. I'm not picking up on that at all."

"Maybe it's a boggart," he suggested, a note of hope in his voice. It had long been Mr. Malone's dearest wish to confront one of these mischievous creatures, although he had been thwarted by the fact they were said to live mostly in Scotland, a country he had yet to visit.

"No, I'm getting something more like . . . hmm, it feels like . . . yes, a restless spirit! Trapped on the earthly plane, unable to move on!" said Mrs. Malone.

"Oh, please," said Franny, "not another restless spirit." She had wrapped a dish towel around her head and was leaning against the wall, moodily nibbling a cracker. "They always turn out to be a loose shutter or a trapped squirrel or something, and we always end up looking like complete idiots."

"Not always," said Mr. Malone. He was drumming his fingers on the windowsill, clearly thinking hard. "That investigation in Baltimore—"

"That was the worst!" said Franny. "If we hadn't moved to Florida, I'd still have kids calling me 'Freaky Franny' and making those stupid '*whooo*' noises when I walked down the hallway."

"Well, you keep saying you want to be a movie star," said Will. "Don't you like being the center of attention and having everyone talking about you?"

Franny gave him a withering look. "Yes," she

said, "if they are talking about my *acting*. But instead, they're gossiping about my weird family—"

"Franny," said her mother. "We don't use that word."

Franny crossed her arms, slid down to the floor, and stared sulkily at the ceiling. "My life," she told the cracked plaster, "is beyond tragic."

"Nonsense, it will give you something to talk about in interviews once you're famous," said Mr. Malone. He returned to trying to open the window, although his mind was clearly distracted. "A restless spirit," he mused. "That covers a lot of ground. It could be a murder victim or someone who died with unfinished business—"

"Hey, maybe the house was built on the site of an ancient burial ground!" Will said with the earnest, wide-eyed expression of a choirboy. "Wouldn't that be *awesome*?"

Will winked at Poppy, who crossed her eyes at him again. She felt quite strongly that their parents didn't need any encouragement, even if it was sarcastic. They never noticed the sarcasm, anyway;

they always thought their children were showing a sincere interest in their work. If anything, Poppy thought, someone needed to dampen their enthusiasm on a regular basis.

"There's an idea!" said Mrs. Malone. "We've never investigated a graveyard curse before."

"It would be good experience for us," Mr. Malone agreed. "Broaden our scope a bit. We should get the magnetometer out of the trunk of the car, do a few readings after dinner."

"I have to recalibrate it," said Poppy. "It's been wonky ever since Will dropped it when we were chasing that cow through the swamp—"

"When we were chasing Bigfoot through the swamp," her father corrected her automatically.

"We never found any evidence that it was Bigfoot," she protested.

"And we never found any evidence that it wasn't," he replied.

"Dad," Poppy said. "It *mooed*."

"For all we know, that's Bigfoot's mating call," he said, dismissing this with a wave of his hand.

"If you want to be a scientist, Poppy, you must learn to keep an open mind."

She had just opened her mouth to protest when her father turned back to the window with renewed energy. He gave an extra hard push on the sash, the window flew up with a bang, and he fell backward onto the floor.

"Ow," he said, blinking at the ceiling.

"You see?" Mrs. Malone said triumphantly to the room. "A Dark Presence, hard at work." She sighed happily. "We are going to have *such fun*."

Chapter
TWO

If there was a Dark Presence haunting their new home, the good news was that it had plenty of room to lurk about.

After the Malones had bandaged their various wounds, they began to explore the house, which had been provided at a very low rent as part of Mr. and Mrs. Malone's grant.

It had been built more than a hundred years ago. It was large and square, with a front staircase in the living room and a creaky back staircase in the kitchen. The main floor had a parlor with cabbage rose wallpaper, which Mrs. Malone instantly claimed as her study, and a small room half hidden off the kitchen that Mr. Malone staked out as his office, saying that it had been so hard to find that he was certain to have peace and quiet at last.

The second floor had eight bedrooms which, although they were small and oddly shaped—one was actually triangular—pleased all the Malones enormously.

"No more sharing rooms!" said Franny, who had begun clamoring for a room of her own (preferably with private bathroom attached) as soon as she turned thirteen.

"And no more sleeping on the couch when people come to stay," added Will, who had often been turned out of his bed for guests.

Narrow steps led to the third floor, which contained two more small bedrooms and a large attic area where all the Malones' investigating equipment could be stored.

"What a lot of space," Mrs. Malone said happily once they had all gathered again in the living room. "Did you see all those high ceilings! They offer such a feeling of light and airiness, don't you think?"

"I'm getting more of a feeling of draftiness," said Mr. Malone. "And of astronomical heating bills come December."

"Oh, I've read that it's very mild here in the winter," said Mrs. Malone. "And it will be so nice to offer our visitors their own bedrooms instead of pull-out couches in the basement."

Mr. Malone looked, if possible, even gloomier. In his college days, before he had met Mrs. Malone, he had founded an organization called the Paranormal Society of Investigators, or PSI. His plan had been basically to pad his résumé in order to get better jobs and to attract members who would fork over enough dues to pay for part of his rent and an occasional spaghetti dinner in town. In return, they received an infrequent newsletter (badly printed and full of misspellings) with news and gossip from the small world of parapsychologists.

Then he met and married Mrs. Malone. Within months, the newsletter began appearing regularly (nicely designed and with every word spelled correctly), and she had embarked on lengthy correspondences with many of PSI's members. She encouraged them when their investigations failed, cheered for them when they won grants or landed jobs, and offered them a place to stay when they were passing through town and had spent their last dime on a new ectoplasm detector or digital recorder.

"I must remember to put our new address in the next newsletter," she said.

"Why don't we just register as a bed-and-breakfast while we're at it?" Mr. Malone said. "We'll never get any peace. The doorbell will be ringing at all hours of the day and night—"

Just then, as if to prove his point, the doorbell rang.

"You see?" he said. "This is how it begins! The hordes of locusts are descending. And we don't even have any furniture yet!"

Fortunately, the person ringing the bell was not a roving parapsychologist but the driver of the moving van.

"This the Malone house?" he asked. "Where do you want me to put the cauldron?"

Poppy knew, of course, that her family was easily distracted, especially when there was work to be done. Still, she had hoped that this move would be different. She had hoped that everyone would pitch in cheerfully to unpack boxes, hang curtains, make beds, buy food, and generally manage to get things organized some time before Christmas. But once again, her hopes were dashed.

No one was doing any of those useful and practical things. Instead, her mother had started digging through boxes of books, hoping to find the volume that she vaguely remembered had an interesting chapter about cursed burial grounds. Her father was furiously reading over the bill from the moving company and making angry notes about what he planned to say when he called them in the morning. Franny had retired to the bathroom to dry her hair. Rolly, who had been discouraged from tearing up the kitchen floor, had taken his fork outside to dig up flowers instead. And Will was lying on the couch, his eyes closed and his hands peacefully folded over his chest.

"Will! Wake up! You can't take a nap while the rest of us are working," Poppy said, overstating the case a bit since, actually, no one besides her was doing anything helpful.

"I'm not taking a nap," he said in a dreamy, faraway voice. "I think perhaps . . . yes . . . I feel a trance coming on."

"Really?" Mrs. Malone straightened up from her box of books and hurried over to peer down at him. "How exciting!"

"How convenient, you mean," said Poppy. "He always happens to fall into a trance when there's work to do."

"I cannot control the timing," whispered Will. "The visions just . . . appear."

"Can you describe what you're seeing, dear?" Mrs. Malone asked in a hushed voice. "Wouldn't it be wonderful if you were receiving a mental transmission from Deodat; he promised to take part in my remote viewing experiment when he went to India." She glanced at her watch. "Of course, it's a little after midnight over there, but Deo always was a night owl—"

"Mom, Will's taking a nap," protested Poppy.

"Going into a trance," murmured Will.

"Mom—" Poppy began, but her mother held up her hand.

"Don't disturb your brother," Mrs. Malone whispered. "Perhaps this time Deo will finally get through." She leaned closer and said, "Can you describe what you see, Will?"

Will lifted one languid hand and covered his eyes. "It's very fuzzy," he said. "Just a shining white object . . . kind of round, I think . . . big at the bottom, pointy at the top . . ."

"The Taj Mahal!" Mrs. Malone cried, beaming.

"Or a turnip," Poppy said. "Get *up*."

She kicked the couch leg and was immediately sorry.

"Poppy, if you can't be quiet, please unpack

something," said her mother said. "Deo will simply never break through if you keep yelling and hopping about."

Poppy limped up two flights of stairs, feeling disgruntled and misunderstood and ill-treated. Will's supposed talent for remote viewing had started a year ago, during a particularly rainy month. The search for Bigfoot had been put on hold, thanks to rising swamp waters, so Mr. and Mrs. Malone had subjected their children to a series of experiments that could be conducted indoors. They had spent days sitting around the living room, trying to read one another's thoughts and move objects with their minds.

When that got boring—their minds were apparently complete mysteries to one another and the only object that ever moved was a walnut that Will surreptiously flicked with a finger— Mrs. Malone had called a PSI member who lived in San Francisco and asked him to sit in front of a city landmark for an hour and concentrate on mentally transmitting a picture of what he saw.

When Will had guessed, correctly, that the man was looking at the Golden Gate Bridge, Mrs. Malone had hugged him and Mr. Malone had beamed with pride.

"I always knew you children had Unseen Talents," Mrs. Malone had cried. "How could you not? You have been raised in an atmosphere that is open to the unknown and the mysterious!"

"Lucky guess," Poppy had hissed in Will's ear.

He had smiled smugly and embarked on a series of remote viewing experiments that involved lying down at convenient moments on beds, couches, porch swings, hammocks, and even, on long road trips, the entire backseat of the car.

Poppy had to admit that Will's strategy was clever. He could get out of washing dishes, mowing the lawn, or being used as a test subject in other experiments simply by going limp and horizontal. She, however, scorned such subterfuge.

This meant that Poppy often found herself doing tedious and unpleasant things such as (she

realized as soon as she opened the attic door)
unpacking boxes of equipment in the stifling heat.

The first thing she did was to throw open the
small window (wishing that her father had been
there to see how easily she had done this). For a
few moments, Poppy gazed at the treetops, imagining that she was looking down on billowing green
ocean waves with an occasional rooftop poking up
like a lonely shingled island. A slight breeze brought
with it the smell of fresh-cut grass and the faint
sound of wind chimes. The neighborhood was so
still and quiet in the golden afternoon light that it
could have been an enchanted town in a fairy tale.

She took a few deep breaths, then turned back
to the attic and the large cardboard boxes labeled
LABORATORY in bold black letters. Poppy opened a box
at random and began taking out equipment and
placing it on a wooden table. First, there was the
desktop computer that her mother used to run ESP
programs, then the three battered laptops that her
parents took into the field. Next, an infrared video
camera, a thermal imager, several mini-digital

recorders. There were a magnetometer to measure fluctuations in the magnetic field and a thermometer to record any sudden and inexplicable drops in temperature. There were a number of regular cameras, plus a half-dozen camera traps that could be set up to take a photo any time a motion detector was tripped.

Poppy opened another box and stared down at a snarl of electrical cords, frowning. She knew she had tied all the equipment cords into tidy bundles when they were packing to move. She clearly remembered this because Will was supposed to do it but he'd made a mess, as usual, and her mother had asked her to straighten it out, also as usual, and she had spent an irritable thirty minutes organizing the cords and wondering exactly when Will had figured out that if he did a chore very badly the first time he was asked, he would never have to do it again.

Sighing, she crouched on the floor and began trying to unknot the cords. Strands of straight brown hair fell into her face and soon beads of sweat trickled down her nose. After managing to untangle several computer cables, she ran into a particularly stubborn knot. She sat cross-legged on the floor to work on it, feeling hotter and sweatier by the minute. Finally, she lost all patience and tugged violently at the end of one of the cords.

That, of course, only pulled the knot tighter.

"Aaggh!" she yelled, tossing the whole mess back into the box. And then, for good measure, she kicked the box to the wall.

That was when she heard it. A snicker, soft but clear, and obviously quite amused.

She turned her head sharply. Her eyes scanned the attic, but all she saw beside the boxes and equipment was an old wooden wardrobe, several trunks covered with dust, and a spider scuttling through a crack in the floor.

She held her breath and listened, but she could only hear an ice cream truck jingling down the street and Franny's voice in the distance, calling out something to their mother.

Poppy shrugged, sat down under the low eaves, and opened another box. She found a half-dozen flashlights and a night-vision scope.

"Yes!" she said. She started to stand up and promptly bumped her head against the eaves.

As she clutched the top of her head in pain, she heard it again. That scratchy chuckle, laughing at her. And then, out of the corner of her eye, she saw a flash of movement by the door. . . .

It's the heat, she thought. I'm having a hallucination.

Slowly and carefully, she took one step, then another.

I'll go downstairs and have a cold glass of water, she told herself. I'll lie down with a wet cloth on my head. And then I'll stop hearing things and see-ing things and—

She glanced into the box of cords and stopped dead in her tracks.

Every single cable and cord, even the ones she had worked so hard to straighten out, were now twisted and knotted together, even worse than before.

This time, when she heard the mocking laugh, Poppy whirled around, scanning the room. And that's when she saw a little man standing in the corner, his pointed white teeth gleaming in the shadows.

Chapter
THREE

Poppy blinked, took a deep breath, and blinked again.

The man was so small that he was half hidden behind a rusty birdcage. He was about two feet tall, with curly white hair and a beard that flowed over a round little belly. He wore a red stocking cap, a moss-green wool coat, brown pants, and boots. He looked, in fact, exactly like a garden gnome.

A wave of relief swept over her. A lawn statue, left behind by a previous owner—of course! The laughter she had heard was simply a crow cawing. That flicker of movement was caused by sweat blurring her vision. The way his little black eyes seemed to glitter in the shadows—that was just a reflection from the bare lightbulb hanging overhead.

There was always a simple, ordinary explanation for any supposedly mysterious occurrence. . . .

And then the little man sneezed. For a panic-stricken second, his eyes met hers. Then he looked away, staring fixedly over her head at the wall.

But it was too late. Once you've heard a lawn statue sneeze, you can't pretend you didn't.

Poppy put her hand on a table for support, feeling that the universe had suddenly swung topsy-turvy. She had spent most of her life arguing with her parents that it was scientifically impossible for ghosts, monsters, or UFOs to exist. Now here she was, facing clear evidence that she, Poppy Malone, was *wrong*.

She knelt down so that she could look into his face. "Don't be scared," she said. "I'm not going to hurt you."

He quit staring at the wall and glared at her. "As if I would be," he responded scornfully. "As if you could!"

She rocked back on her heels. "You can talk!"

"Let me guess," he said sarcastically. "You must be the smart one."

She stood up so suddenly that the blood rushed from her head, leaving her dizzy. She grabbed the edge of the table again and tried to figure out how to ask the question that was occupying her mind without sounding rude.

Finally, she just blurted it out. "What *are* you?"

A cunning look slid across his face. "Sure and I'm a leprechaun," he said. His accent was terrible. He sounded like Mr. Martin, her principal from three schools ago, who insisted on delivering morning announcements in a fake Irish brogue on St. Patrick's Day.

He began to sidle along the wall with an elaborately unconcerned look on his face. "And now that ye've caught me, I have to give ye my pot of gold. . . ."

"Yeah, right," Poppy said. "There's no such thing as leprechauns—"

If it hadn't been for her brief and bruising stint as the fourth-grade soccer goalie, he would have vanished between one blink and the next. But she saw his eyes shift to one side, and she managed to get between him and the door just in time.

"Grwtchz!" he cursed. (At least it sounded very much like a curse to her.)

"I suppose next you'll try to tell me you're an elf," she said, disgusted.

"An elf?" He stopped trying to slip past her. He stood with his hands on his hips and glared up at her. "An *elf*?! Do I *look* cute? Do I *look* cheerful? Do I *look* like I have a brain filled with rainbows and moonbeams?"

"I was just *asking*—"

"Could an elf do this?" he cried, flinging out his hand dramatically.

An instant later, she heard a series of loud pops that sounded like firecrackers going off. The attic lightbulb burst with a flash of light. The sound of Franny's blow-dryer stopped abruptly, and a hush fell as every fan in the house wheezed to a stop.

For a long moment, there was only silence.

Then it was broken by Franny's despairing wail and her father's voice floating up the stairs. "Must have blown a fuse . . . these old houses . . . I'll check the basement. . . ."

"Ha!" The little man chuckled with satisfaction. "*I* happen to be a goblin."

Poppy stared at him. She could hear a dog barking in the distance, a lawn mower purring next door, a bird singing in a tree outside. She focused on these everyday, ordinary sounds for the space of three breaths, then she repeated, as matter-of-factly as possible, "A goblin. Right." Without taking her eyes off him, she reached out one hand to take a camera out of one of the boxes.

His black eyes glittered with sudden alarm. "And just what do you think you're going to do with that?"

"Take your picture, of course," she said calmly. She glanced down at the viewfinder and saw the goblin's brown boots. Then the screen turned a blurry pink, and she looked up to see that the goblin had put his hand firmly in front of the camera lens, like a celebrity trying to ward off a pesky photographer.

"Who do you think you are, pointing that thing at me without even asking?" he asked.

"Fine." She sighed. "May I take your picture?"

"What's the magic word?"

She ground her teeth, but forced herself to say, "May I *please* take your picture?"

"No," he answered briskly. "Now put that thing away."

Annoyed, she lifted the camera and looked through the viewfinder.

"It's just a photo," she said. "Just for my records."

He screwed up his face. "Oh, right," he said. "As if we haven't heard that one before! You know, my Great-uncle Murk once let someone take a photo of him. 'Just as a memento,' the man said. 'Just to show my kids.' Next thing you know, Uncle Murk was a sideshow attraction in a traveling circus! Took him three years to escape and he was never the same again. Twitched any time he heard calliope music, developed an allergy to cotton candy, just hearing the word *elephant* was enough to send him to his bed for days—"

"I'm not going to sell you to a circus," Poppy said, exasperated. "Honestly. What kind of a person do you think I am?"

He gave her a dark look. "A *human* person."

"I promise I won't let anyone see it," she said, pointing the camera again.

She stepped back to get a better shot. Unfortunately, she forgot about the packing box on the floor right behind her. She regained her balance just in time to see the very tip of the goblin's red stocking cap as he escaped through the door.

"Will! Franny! Stop him!" Poppy yelled as she clattered down the stairs.

But Franny's hair dryer was once again roaring behind the bathroom door, and Will was now snoring on the couch. Poppy jumped over the last three steps and burst through the front door, but she already knew that she was too late and too slow. The goblin dashed toward the corner of the house. Her only chance to catch him was about to vanish. . . .

Then she heard a baby yell something that sounded like "Ack-ja!" and the goblin skidded to a stop in front of the flower garden. He flipped up his red stocking cap so that it pointed straight to the sky, and then he froze with his arms at his sides and a fixed smile on his face.

Puzzled, Poppy looked from the goblin to the sidewalk, where she saw a man pushing a stroller. He was looking straight ahead, deep in conversation on his cell phone. The baby in the stroller, however, was staring in her direction.

"Ack-jubba-ju," the baby gabbled, pointing insistently at the goblin.

"I'll call you back," the baby's father said into the phone. "Jordan's trying to get my attention."

He followed his baby's pointing finger and saw Poppy. "Hey, there," he said, smiling. "Just moved in?"

"Yes, this morning," she said. "My name's Poppy Malone."

He nodded in a friendly way and said, "Nice to

meet you. I'm Alan from two doors down, and this is Jordan—"

"Oh-SI!" Jordan shrieked.

"Nice gnome," Alan-from-two-doors-down added vaguely just as his cell phone rang again. He flipped it open, nodded to Poppy, said, "See you around," and walked on, lost in his conversation once more. His baby, on the other hand, stared at the gnome until his stroller was out of sight.

"Pox and postules!" the goblin said, flipping his stocking cap back down. "Spotted again! Twice in one day! I must be losing my touch—"

He stopped in mid-sentence and stared past her. A tiny smile curled the edge of his mouth; his eyes softened and his expression looked almost tender.

"Hel-lo," he said softly. "Who's this, then?"

Poppy turned her head a careful half-inch, keeping one eye on the goblin in case this was another trick.

Rolly, dressed in nothing but underpants and a sequined sombrero, was trotting toward a ladder that was leaning against the house. He was humming tunelessly and carrying a spatula and a jar of peanut butter.

After carefully climbing five rungs, he took a long, appraising look at the window closest to the ladder. Then he scooped an enormous glop of peanut butter from the jar and began coating the window screen with all the care of a Renaissance painter creating a masterpiece.

Poppy heard the goblin draw in a sharp breath. "I don't think I've ever seen anyone do that before," he said.

"Of course you haven't," she said sharply. "Because only Rolly would think of it."

"Rol-lee." The goblin said the name slowly, as if savoring the taste of it. "And who is Rolly?"

"My little brother." Poppy didn't like the goblin's expression. She didn't like the way his small dark eyes glittered with interest as he stared at Rolly, she didn't like the note of curiosity in his voice, and she didn't like the way he was bouncing on his toes as if he was holding a happy secret deep inside his heart.

The goblin grinned.

A goblin's grin, Poppy discovered, was a terrible thing.

"Brilliance," the goblin said under his breath as he watched Rolly deliberately layer more peanut butter on the window screen. "Sheer brilliance."

Now Poppy was feeling really uneasy. "Look," she said. "Whatever you're thinking of doing, you can just forget it—"

Then she saw Rolly reach too far and begin to lose his balance. Without thinking, she ran forward and caught him, then fell backward into a small rosebush.

She opened her mouth, but only managed a strangled moan. Rolly had landed squarely on her stomach, knocking the wind out of her.

"Let me *go*," Rolly said, squirming. He gave a sudden wild wiggle. "I wasn't doing anything wrong."

Poppy caught her breath and managed to stand up. She scanned the yard for the goblin, but she knew it was hopeless. He was long gone.

Rolly made another lunge for freedom, and Poppy grabbed the back of his underpants just in time. "Did you see him? That little man? Where did he go?"

Rolly twisted around in order to stare up into her face. "I didn't see anyone."

"He was standing right there," she insisted, pointing at the flowerbed. "He was about this tall, with a pointy red hat and a white beard. . . ."

Confronted with Rolly's unblinking gaze, Poppy trailed off. Maybe she was suffering from heatstroke, maybe she was discombobulated by the move, maybe she had, in fact, been imagining things after all. . . .

Her sudden attack of doubt made her loosen her grip on Rolly, who instantly gave one particularly wild wiggle, broke free, and headed back to the ladder with a determined look on his face.

"If you start peanut buttering the screen again, I'm going to tell Mom," Poppy said absently, preoccupied with the delicate job of untangling herself from the rosebush's thorny branches (naturally,

Rolly hadn't gotten a scratch). As she gingerly pulled a particularly prickly strand away from her shorts, Poppy glanced down at the flowerbed.

Clearly outlined in the dirt were two tiny footprints.

She froze, her mind racing. Where was the plaster of paris packed? If she could find it, she could make a cast of the footprints—or no, that might take too long. She should get her camera, take some photos, start an investigation file, make sketches in her logbook. . . .

"Rolly, what are you *doing*?" Poppy looked up to see her mother standing on the porch, looking exasperated. "Get *down* from there and come inside the house this minute!"

Rolly gave a little grunt of displeasure—the closest he would ever come to acknowledging a direct order—but he climbed down the ladder and headed slowly and reluctantly for the porch.

"Why in the world would you decide to climb a ladder?" Mrs. Malone continued, a little calmer now that Rolly was safely on the ground. "You could fall and hurt yourself! And as for smearing peanut butter on a window screen—!" She stopped, apparently at a loss for words.

"I wanted birds to come to the window," said Rolly, "and they like peanut butter."

Mrs. Malone's frown was replaced by a radiant smile. "There you go! That's a wonderful example of logical thinking, Rolly." She raised a warning eyebrow and added, "Of course, you should always ask before you put any kind of foodstuff on the house, dear."

Rolly shrugged.

"Now come inside," Mrs. Malone continued. "I have some candy for you. . . ."

Although Rolly didn't often show outright emotion of any kind, he broke into a run at this.

"Wait, stop, *no*!" Poppy yelled, but it was too late.

Rolly ran right through the flowerbed and up the porch steps, neatly destroying the goblin's footsteps on his way.

Chapter
FOUR

Goblin sighting

June 12, 2:46 P.M.

Attic at 1219 Arden Lane, Austin, Texas

Witness: Poppy Malone

Poppy chewed on the end of her pen and stared dubiously at the entry she had just made in her logbook. She had taken a bath, put on her pajamas, and was now sitting cross-legged on her bed. The only light in the room was the warm yellow glow of a bedside lamp, which made everything seem cozy and ordinary and real. She looked around her room, as if to impress upon herself how plain and ordinary and everyday it was. Looking at the lamp and the familiar flowery curtains and the rumpled quilt on her bed (with the ink stain in the corner from the time she fell asleep while writing in her logbook), it seemed impossible to believe that she had actually seen a goblin.

But then she would close her eyes and try to recall every detail of what had happened in the attic, remembering the dull tomato red of the goblin's cap and the scratchy sound of his voice and the way the lightbulbs all popped at once (and she couldn't deny that her father had to replace a fuse; he had complained about it all during dinner). That had all seemed absolutely real, so much so that when she opened her eyes again, the outlines of her bed and dresser and window seemed as hazy and insubstantial as a dream.

She tapped her pen against the page, frowning. Poppy didn't like feeling unsure about what was real and what wasn't.

After much thought, she scratched out what she had written and added a new heading: "Alleged Goblin Sighting."

After a little more thought, she underlined *alleged* several times. Nothing was proven until she had evidence. She had learned that lesson years ago, when she was in kindergarten, and she wasn't likely to forget it.

It had been late in the afternoon, just when shadows begin sliding out from under trees. She had gone down to the creek that ran behind their house in Madison, Indiana. There was a weeping willow tree there, and she liked to hide under the branches and pretend she was in a little house with green, leafy walls.

She was lying on her back, staring at the bits of sky she could see between the leaves, when suddenly something darted in front of her eyes. She waved her hand frantically, thinking it was a wasp, and almost knocked the tiny creature to the ground.

But she didn't, and the fairy hovered for a moment in midair, giving Poppy an incredulous look, as if she were just as astonished to see Poppy as Poppy was to see her. (Poppy had always felt sure that when the fairy had returned home, her story of seeing an actual human being—"Really, I did! I was *this close* to it!"—was probably laughed at, too.) Then Poppy's mother had called to her to come in to dinner, breaking the spell, and the fairy had turned her back and flown off.

Poppy's parents had taken her sighting quite seriously. In fact, they had said several times how pleased and proud they were of her, and talked of setting up a special motion-sensor camera to see if they could catch the fairy on film.

So when Poppy stood in front of her kindergarten class the next day for show-and-tell, she had, quite naturally, decided to talk about what she had seen.

The reaction was not what she had expected. They had all laughed at her.

"Pop-py sees fair-ies," a boy named Vince had chanted until Poppy was almost in tears.

"I did!" Poppy said. "Come over to my house and I'll show you!"

"You'll probably just hang a fairy ornament on a tree and say it's real," a girl named Annette had said. "That's what my daddy says your daddy does. He tricks people."

"He does not!" Poppy had never felt so furious in her whole life (although admittedly she was only five years old). "You're lying."

"Am not."

"Are too."

The discussion went downhill from there. Finally, Miss DuMarch told everyone to be quiet and sit down. Everyone did, although Poppy and Annette glared at each other and Vince kept muttering his chant, just softly enough so that Miss DuMarch could pretend not to hear.

Instead, she said, in a sugary voice, "Now, children, we all know how much fun it is to pretend, don't we? We all love to make believe, isn't that right? So if Poppy wants to pretend that she saw a fairy, it's not really lying. She's just using her imagination to make up a little story. And speaking of stories, why don't we all settle down and I'll read a few more pages of the book we started yesterday. . . ."

* * *

Poppy felt her cheeks get hot just remembering the other children's sidelong glances after Miss DuMarch's betrayal. She began flipping through her logbook, stopping at random pages to read her entries. Over the years, she had recorded one ridiculous investigation after another.

There was that UFO sighting two years ago in Kansas City, for instance. More than forty people called 911 to report a disc-shaped object moving at extremely high speed through the night sky, occasionally making dramatic reverses and turns completely unlike those attainable in an ordinary aircraft.

That, of course, had turned out to be a radio-controlled UFO model operated by a high school prankster. He had finally confessed, but not before Mr. and Mrs. Malone had set up special equipment on the city hall roof, photographed the UFO, and shown the evidence they had collected at a triumphant news conference.

Shortly after the hoax was uncovered, Mr. and Mrs. Malone lost their foundation grants. They weren't suspected of fraud; the foundation investi-gated and concluded that they were simply unwit-ting dupes. Still, it wasn't good to have unwitting dupes on the payroll, either. The Malones were politely asked to move on.

Poppy sighed. She had liked Kansas City. The school cafeteria had chocolate pudding every Friday, there was a public swimming pool three blocks from their house, and the next-door neigh-bor raised golden retrievers and used to let her play with the puppies.

She turned more pages.

Oh yes, there was the werewolf that turned out to be an enormous (and enormously shaggy) stray dog.

And the lake monster that ended up being a mossy, half-submerged log.

And the mysterious cold spot in a supposedly haunted hotel that was nothing more than a bad draft.

Poppy tossed her logbook on the floor, disgusted. How could she have fooled herself into thinking, even for a moment, that goblins really existed?

The pattern was clear. Every single case the Malones had investigated had turned out to have a natural and logical explanation. Really, she thought, what were the odds that her goblin would be any different?

She flopped back on her bed and stared at the ceiling. Goblins belonged in fairy tales and fantasy books and animated movies. Definitely not in real life.

True, there had been discoveries of small, humanlike skeletons over the years. Poppy kept track; she clipped articles and put them in her files. Each new finding was greeted with cries of astonishment and delight as newspapers around the world trumpeted the news that evidence had been found that elves (or gnomes or hobbits) actually existed.

Unfortunately, the evidence never stood up under scrutiny. Most of the time, the remains turned out to be those of lemurs, small primates whose skeletons looked enough like tiny people to fool a few scientists and most reporters.

The odds, Poppy felt, were very much against the existence of goblins.

And yet, she had seen something. Someone. She had talked to him and he had talked back.

If goblins did exist . . .

She turned over onto her stomach. If they did exist, she needed evidence. She had learned an extremely valuable lesson from Miss DuMarch, Annette, and Vince: Never talk about what you've seen until you have absolute proof.

Of course, this goblin—if that, indeed, is what he was—seemed very clever, very cunning. If she were going to match wits with him, she would have to set her trap quite carefully indeed. . . .

Poppy felt the corner of her mouth turn up and realized that she was smiling.

Chapter
FIVE

Poppy stayed up past midnight plotting. When she finally dropped off to sleep, it was to dream of goblins tiptoeing around the house, hiding behind bushes and snickering as she walked by.

The next morning, she got up early, went to the attic, and opened the box that held her parents' camera traps. Each trap had an infrared sensor that detected movement and triggered the camera to take a photo. The cameras were usually used to snap pictures of animals in the wild, but Mr. Malone lived in hope of capturing a candid picture of Bigfoot.

The key to setting a camera trap, Poppy knew, was knowing something about animal habits. A creek where animals might stop to drink, a clump of bushes with berries to eat, an oak tree that dropped hundreds of acorns—these were all good spots to set up a trap because animals would probably wander by and trip the motion sensor.

But what kind of habits did a goblin have? Where did goblins like to go? Well, there was the attic, of course. That was where she'd first spotted him. She should definitely set up a camera trap in the attic.

And there was that big oak tree on the side lawn, the one that the goblin had run past when he made his escape. He looked as if he knew where he was going. Poppy was willing to bet that he was taking a familiar route.

Where else?

Maybe the kitchen, Poppy thought. She had a feeling that the goblin had dumped that bag of flour on Franny's head.

So, good. She had three places to set up her camera traps. Poppy sat back on her heels and considered the geography of the attic. When she had first seen the goblin, he was standing near the stairs, but surely he hadn't entered the attic that way; it was too likely that he would have been seen.

The window was a possibility—although it was high off the ground; it seemed that that would make it difficult for a creature that was only two feet high to get in and out. And another thing . . . She went to the window and looked down. Yes, her memory was correct. There was no helpful trellis on this side of the house to serve as a ladder, no drainpipe to shimmy up and down, no ivy to offer footholds.

A slight frown creased Poppy's forehead. So how had he gotten in?

She was sitting at the desk contemplating this question when the attic door swung open and Will appeared, his cheek still creased from his pillow.

"Hey, Mom says breakfast is ready," he said, yawning. His glance fell on the camera trap, and some of the sleepiness disappeared from his eyes. He grinned slightly. "What's all this?"

"Nothing," Poppy replied, trying to sound nonchalant.

"Poppy, Poppy, Poppy." Will sighed, shaking his head in pretended sorrow. "I thought we had an agreement. I thought we'd made a pact." He sat on the table, his legs swinging, and grinned at her. "Never volunteer to help Mom and Dad with an investigation. It only encourages them."

She pushed a damp strand of hair behind her ear. "You know we're going to get roped into investigating the Dark Presence, whether we like it or not," she said. "I just thought I might as well get it over with, that's all."

He raised his eyebrows at that. "Okay," he said. "Just so long as you don't start believing in all that spooky stuff."

"Will." Poppy gave him a level look. "I'm a scientist, remember?"

"Yeah, well, so are Mom and Dad," he said. "Being a scientist doesn't mean you're not wacko."

"I wouldn't call them wacko," Poppy said weakly, feeling disloyal. "Enthusiastic, maybe . . ."

"That's one word for it," said Will. "Another word is delusional. They've been researching the paranormal for almost twenty years and they've come up with nothing. And yet they won't give up."

Poppy focused her attention on the camera. "It *is* kind of weird," she said carefully. "I mean, I stopped thinking that ghosts were real when I was five. . . ."

"Oh yeah?" He grinned at her. "I seem to remember you screaming pretty loudly last year when we were on that cemetery stakeout."

"A mouse ran over my foot," Poppy said with great dignity. "It took me by surprise." She hesitated, then said quickly, "You don't ever wonder whether things like ghosts or aliens really exist, do you?"

"Oh, sure I do," he said.

She glanced up at him sharply. "Really?"

"Yeah," he said, smirking. "Just like I stay up on Christmas Eve, trying to hear reindeer on the roof."

Poppy made herself return his grin. "Right. Or

search for the end of a rainbow and that pot full of gold coins—"

"Will! Poppy!" Their mother's voice floated up from the kitchen. "The kitchen is about to close!"

Will pushed himself off the table, his sneakers landing on the wooden floor with a thump. "Come on. I'm starving."

"Yeah, okay," Poppy said, giving up for now on the camera trap. She'd have to come back later and see if she could figure out where to set it up.

But as Will was heading toward the stairs, he suddenly stopped and peered more closely at the rusty birdcage. "Hey, look." He moved the birdcage out of the way, revealing a small door by the baseboard. It was about two feet square and painted the same color as the wall. "What's this?"

Before Poppy could answer, he pulled it open, revealing a dark space.

"It must be some kind of ventilation system," Poppy said, trying to sound calm even though her heart had started beating faster.

Will wasn't listening. He knelt down so that

his face was next to the open door. "Helloooo," he called out, his voice echoing hollowly.

There was a sudden loud clatter from the kitchen as if someone had dropped a pan.

Will turned his head and winked at Poppy. "Listen to this," he whispered. He turned back to the opening and made a long, loud groaning noise.

"Emerson!" They could hear their mother's voice in the kitchen, high-pitched with excitement. "Did you hear that? We may be having another manifestation!"

Will grinned. "What do you think I should say next? Maybe something like, 'Beware'?" He deepened his voice and stretched the word out— "*Beeeewaaare!*"—so that he sounded like a ghostly special effect in a horror movie. "Or how about 'Get *ooouuut*!'?"

Poppy grabbed Will's shoulder and pulled him away from the wall. "Talk about getting them all worked up! If you keep making those kinds of noises, we'll be stuck in this house all summer, trying to make recordings of electronic voice phenomena and staring at electromagnetic field detectors!"

His smile vanished. "Oh."

There seemed to be a sudden burst of activity downstairs. "Where's the digital recorder?" Mr. Malone called out. "Lucille, could you catch any words?"

"I'd better go down and tell them it was just me." Will sighed. "I feel terrible. It's like telling a kid there's no tooth fairy. . . ."

Poppy waited until she was sure that her brother had made it to the bottom of the stairs. Then she cut a small hole in the side of one of the moving boxes, set the camera trap inside, and turned the box so that the camera lens pointed at the tiny door in the wall.

On her way downstairs, she turned back to examine her work. She nodded in satisfaction. No one, not even a goblin, would see anything except a plain, ordinary, boring cardboard box.

* * *

The rest of the afternoon passed in a blur of box unpacking and furniture arranging, thanks to Mrs. Malone's tiresome insistence that they get the house in order before moving on to more interesting pursuits, such as going swimming at the Barton Springs Pool (Will's suggestion), exploring the neighborhood (Franny's), or heading to the library to research likely candidates for the Dark Presence (Mr. Malone's).

Despite the definite whiff of mutiny in the air, Mrs. Malone prevailed simply by fixing them all with a stern gaze and saying, "If we don't do this now, we'll be living out of boxes until Christmas. And I am not going to let everyone leave me to do all the unpacking . . . again."

"When have we ever done that?" Mr. Malone protested feebly.

Mrs. Malone snorted and pointed to a large box marked FILES. "Those are all yours, Emerson," she said. "Will can help you carry them to your study."

Will gave the box—which was almost the size of a refrigerator—a martyred look. "Why didn't the movers put it Dad's study in the first place?" he asked. "That thing probably weighs two thousand pounds."

"Don't exaggerate, Will; it's just a box of papers. And those movers clearly had no idea where anything should go." She looked with displeasure at the box full of pots and pans left in the middle of the living room floor, the jewelry box placed in the empty fireplace, and the toaster perched on top of the china cabinet. "Franny, Poppy, I want you two to pick up anything that's not in the right place and put it someplace where it belongs. Once we've got the smaller things sorted out, we can start figuring out where to put the couch and coffee table—"

"Really, I think that I'll be more useful at the library, getting started on our research—" Mr. Malone began. He stopped short at the sight of Rolly marching toward the front door carrying a small plastic bucket and spade.

"Hold on there," he said, so firmly that even Rolly's purposeful step faltered. "Where are you going and what's in that bucket?"

"Nothing," said Rolly. Natural prudence prevented him from adding, ". . . yet." Instead, he held out the empty bucket for his father's inspection.

"You're not going to dig for worms, are you?" asked Mr. Malone.

"No," Rolly said with perfect truth, since he'd given up on worms and planned to search for maggots instead.

"I don't think we should put restrictions on his curiosity, dear—"

"Oh, of course not!" Mr. Malone said, his voice rising. "Far be it from me to dampen his enthusiasm for non-arthropod invertebrates! When I think of how close I came to getting a brilliant teaching job and how That Boy ruined it all—"

"Any child might wonder whether worms can swim," said Mrs. Malone said. "Any bright, imaginative, curious child with an innate understanding of the scientific method, that is."

"Swim, yes," Mr. Malone snapped. "But swim in tomato soup? Soup that is about to be served at a dinner party for the dean of a prestigious university who I am trying to impress so that I can get a job and keep my family out of the poorhouse?" His voice had increased in volume until he was almost shouting. The Incident of the Wormy Soup had happened a year ago, but Mr. Malone's memory had clearly not dimmed.

"Most fathers would be delighted by the prospect of educating a child like Rolly," said Mrs. Malone. "I keep saying that we should have him tested; he's probably a genius. I wouldn't be surprised if he grew up to be a Nobel Prize winner someday—"

"Or a criminal mastermind," Mr. Malone muttered darkly.

"Emerson!" Mrs. Malone nodded meaningfully at Rolly. "Please. You know how sensitive he is."

"Sensitive! Ha!" said Mr. Malone. "That Boy is impervious to public opinion."

Mrs. Malone peered over her glasses, frowning, and said, "Which only proves my point! That is a common characteristic of geniuses. . . ."

This argument could have continued for some time had Rolly not decided to make a break for the great outdoors.

It took all three of his siblings to thwart his escape: Will to grab Rolly as he darted toward the door, Franny to help hold him down, and Poppy to coax him to stay inside.

"We don't have time to watch over you," she said to him, neatly moving her foot aside before he could bite her ankle. "We have to work right now, but I promise we'll play with you later."

"You always say that." Rolly panted, unsuccessfully trying to break free from Will, who had decided to put his time to good use by practicing a wrestling hold. "And you never do."

"Let him go, Will, please," said Mrs. Malone. "This isn't a gym. Rolly, come over here and sit on the couch and I'll get you a nice book to look at. . . ."

After a short, spirited argument, Rolly was finally persuaded to sit on the couch with volume P–R of the encyclopedia set that Mrs. Malone had been given as a child. He quickly became absorbed in the illustrations and diagrams that accompanied an article on pyrotechnics.

The rest of the Malones, sighing and grumbling, got to work.

Several hours later, the furniture had finally been placed, the rugs unrolled, the curtains hung, the clothes unpacked. The only thing left was to figure out where to put all the interesting objects that had been collected by the Malones during their travels.

Some had been picked up by Mr. and Mrs. Malone during the early days of their marriage, and they were quite sentimental about them.

The cauldron, alleged to be an actual piece of evidence seized in the Salem witch trials, was set in its usual place of pride beside the fireplace.

The jars of mummy powder had been given to Mr. and Mrs. Malone on their wedding trip to Egypt by a professor who had been researching local rumors that mummies had a habit of leaving their pyramids and walking about at night. Mrs. Malone decided to line them on a windowsill in the kitchen, reasoning that the jars—which ranged from blue to turquoise to sea-green violet—would look very pretty in the morning light.

The twisted and burned piece of metal, covered with strange, undecipherable writing, ended up on the fireplace mantel. Will claimed to have found this on a camping trip near Roswell, New Mexico, the town where a UFO was supposed to have crashed in 1947. This had always seemed unlikely, given that the camping trip had taken place more than fifty years later, but Will was adamant that the metal object—whatever it was—would serve as a useful conversation piece.

The nineteenth-century photos of séances—filled with people wearing stiff, old-fashioned clothes and ghosts wearing nothing but filmy ecto-plasm—were hung in the front hall. Franny care-fully lined up her collection of voodoo dolls on one of the bookshelves (she had long ago stopped playing with dolls, of course, but could never quite summon up the nerve to give these away).

The witch's broomstick from Cornwall was

tucked in a corner; the haunted Victrola was placed beside the front window; the ESP cards, previously owned by famed parapsychologist Dr. F.H.W. Richardson were reverentially displayed on a side table.

"There," Mrs. Malone said with a sigh of satisfaction. "It's finally beginning to feel like home."

Suddenly, there was a roar from the direction of Mr. Malone's study. "Rolly!" he yelled. The door was flung open and Mr. Malone emerged, his face scarlet. "Where is that blasted boy?"

"Okay, *now* it feels like home," Will murmured from where he was reclining on the rug. (He had rolled it out, as directed, in front of the fireplace. Minutes later, when his mother had suggested that he might want to help her carry a dresser up a flight of stairs, he had suddenly felt faint and had spent ten minutes stretched out on the floor, talking vaguely about visions of bridges and tall buildings.)

"What in the world are you going on about, Emerson?" asked Mrs. Malone.

"That Boy!" He shook a small wooden box pointedly in the air. "He's been pilfering my coins again! Is it too much to expect that a man's property remain safe and secure from theft by his own family?"

The rest of the family was torn between sympathy for this point of view (they had all suffered their own losses, thanks to Rolly's refusal to accept the idea of private ownership of property) and a strong feeling that, in this case, Mr. Malone was largely at fault.

"You shouldn't have told Rolly they were wishing coins," Poppy pointed out.

"I said they were found on the site of an ancient well, commonly believed to grant wishes," Mr. Malone corrected her. "Which is perfectly true—"

"Except you also said there was documented evidence that the wishes came true," said Mrs. Malone. "Who could blame a poor, sweet, innocent little boy—"

"Hello?" Will sat up, blinking owlishly. "I thought we were talking about Rolly?"

"Who could blame him for thinking they were actually magic?" Mrs. Malone finished, ignoring him.

"Remember when we stopped for gas in Oklahoma?" Poppy asked. "Remember when Dad had to pay twenty dollars to get someone to open up the soda machine coin box?"

"I don't know why Rolly didn't simply ask me for the money," Mr. Malone said, momentarily diverted. "It's not as if I'm completely destitute. It's not as if I couldn't spare a few quarters."

"Rolly said he was testing the coins," Will reminded his father. "He wished that he'd get five sodas for the price of one—"

"And the man did give him a free can," Franny said. "So in a way, his wish did come true."

"There, you see!" said Mrs. Malone. "If you would simply try to think the way Rolly does—"

"Now there's a recipe for madness," Mr. Malone muttered. "We don't have time to plumb the inner workings of his mind; we just need to find him."

"It's too hot," Franny complained, collapsing onto the windowseat. "And I'm exhausted."

She flung her head back dramatically, holding one weary hand to her brow.

Will fell back onto the rug and closed his eyes. "I think I'm getting a transmittal," he murmured. "It's big . . . metallic . . . kind of pointy at one end. . . ."

Mr. Malone gave them all a jaded look. "Those coins are going to fund your college educations," he said. "Now fan out before Rolly spends them on a plane ticket to Rio."

So they fanned out, calling Rolly's name.

Poppy didn't waste her breath shouting. She knew that the more frantic they sounded, the more likely it was that Rolly would stay hidden.

Instead, she checked the kind of hiding places he usually liked: under the porch, inside the laundry hamper, behind an overgrown bush. . . .

That was where she spotted a dull glint in the dirt. She peered closer and saw the stern profile of a Roman emperor. She picked up the coin and scanned the ground nearby. A few feet away, another coin lay half hidden in the grass. After that, it was easy to pick up Rolly's trail, which led straight across the yard to the shed.

As Poppy got closer, she could hear Rolly's voice. It sounded as if he was chatting with someone.

This was puzzling. Rolly, as Poppy well knew, didn't particularly enjoy two-way dialogue. He preferred to make short, simple statements that did not encourage any response, argument, or further conversation.

Maybe he's found a friend already, she thought dubiously. Rolly didn't really make friends, either (and when he had been forced to go on playdates, he was usually sent home early with a frosty suggestion that he would be invited back only after he'd been taught not to empty a dozen Jell-O packets into a swimming pool or rappel up the living room curtains).

Poppy opened the shed door and found Rolly sitting next to a rusty lawn mower, spinning one of Mr. Malone's wishing coins on the ground. He looked up at her, blinking in the shaft of sunlight that came through the open door.

He was alone.

"Rolly, you've got to quit taking Dad's coins," said Poppy. "How would you feel if someone took your money?"

"I don't have any," he said. "That's why I took these."

"Yes, I know, but that's not the point. . . ." Faced with Rolly's beady stare, Poppy's voice faltered. "Oh, never mind. Come on, let's go back to the house."

As she helped him to his feet, another coin fell to the ground. Poppy quickly picked it up before Rolly could and added, "If you wouldn't fill your pockets with rocks and twigs and stolen money, you wouldn't get so many holes in them, you know."

She pushed her bangs off her forehead. "So who were you talking to?"

"When?" Rolly asked blankly.

"Just now. I heard you talking when I was standing outside the shed."

A wary expression flitted across his face. "No, you didn't."

"Rolly, I heard you with my own ears," said Poppy. "Who was in here with you?"

His expression became, if possible, even more mulish. "No one."

"Rolly . . ." She narrowed her eyes and stared at him.

He stared right back.

After a very long minute, she gave up. No one in the family had ever won a staring contest with Rolly.

"Okay, fine." She sighed, leading him out of the shed. "Let's go."

But as Poppy and Rolly walked back to the house, she could have sworn she heard a faint snicker coming from the tangle of leaves and twigs behind the shed.

Chapter
SIX

"All right, now, let's get organized," Mr. Malone said briskly. "Poppy and Franny, I want you to set up the thermal-imaging cameras—let's cover as much of the house as we can until we find out where the noise is coming from. Will, go get the electromagnetic field detectors. We'll set those up on the first and second floors. And we need to set up our digital recorders, too, I think. The Dark Presence hasn't spoken yet, but it's early days yet, early days. . . ."

Mr. Malone had spent most of the last three days at the library. Every evening, he would return home brimming with enthusiasm about what he had discovered in the archives. As it turned out, a half-dozen people had died in their house over the years. Even better, three of them had died mysterious, tragic, sensational deaths—just the kind that were the most likely to produce a disgruntled spirit. Now he was busily trying to build excitement for his latest investigation among his family, most of whom were dubious.

"I'm putting my money on Lucinda Greythorn," said Mr. Malone as he positioned a tripod in the center of the living room. "She had the the right profile. Obsessive, overly emotional, clingy. Those kind always linger."

"Which one was Lucinda again?" Will asked, yawning. He was stretched out on a couch by the front window. "The tipsy old lady who fell down the back stairs?"

"She wasn't tipsy, Will; she simply tripped over her cat," said Mrs. Malone. "No, Lucinda was only twenty when she died, poor thing."

"So tragic." Franny sighed as she dreamily attached a camera to a tripod. "Lucinda got engaged to the love of her life just before he enlisted to fight in the Civil War. When they said good-bye, she promised she would always wait for him. And then"—she clasped her hands under her chin and rolled her eyes to the ceiling—"he never returned! Poor Lucinda refused all food and drink until she finally died . . . *of a broken heart.*"

"Or of starvation," said Poppy.

"Poppy!"

"You have to admit that's a more likely cause of death," Poppy said. "If you don't fix that camera, it's going to fall off the tripod again."

"Why do you have to be so practical all the time?" Franny tossed her head; a fine, disdainful gesture that was ruined when she had to lunge forward to catch the camera. "*I* think Lucinda is one of the most romantic people I've ever heard of."

"Well, maybe," said Mrs. Malone. "But dying for love does seem to show a certain lack of . . . spirit, don't you think? One needs ambition and drive to be a Dark Presence. Poor Lucinda sounds as if she was rather *limp.*"

"How about Thaddeus Fuller?" suggested Mr. Malone. "He fought that duel on the front lawn—"

"What a silly thing to do," said Mrs. Malone. "Getting killed over an argument about a duck, of all things."

Will managed to gather enough energy to prop himself up on his elbows and stare out the window. "I wonder if that's where he died," he said, a sudden note of interest in his voice. "I wonder how much blood there was."

"Eww, that is so gross." Franny flipped a blond curl over her shoulder and checked her reflection in the hall mirror. "I'd much rather have Lucinda hanging around the house than Thaddeus."

"You're awfully quiet, Poppy," said Mrs. Malone. "Are you feeling all right?"

"Hmm? Oh, yes, of course." Poppy had been distracted all day, ever since she had arisen early to check her camera traps. The camera on the lawn had a dozen photos on its memory card, but as she had expected, they were all pictures of local cats and dogs, plus several raccoons, a dozen squirrels, and one possum.

The camera in the kitchen had revealed several

shots of her father. The first one showed him entering the kitchen, the second showed him glancing furtively over his shoulder as he opened the refrigerator, and the third captured him sneaking the last piece of chocolate cake.

She had slipped the camera's memory card in her pocket and gone upstairs, her pulse beating faster with every step. She had saved the camera trap in the attic for last, thinking that it offered her the best chance of capturing a picture of a goblin.

As it turned out, there were three photos on the camera's memory card.

The first one showed a blur as the small door in the wall swung open.

The second one showed a slash of red. To Poppy, it looked as if the camera had just managed to catch the tip of a goblin's hat. She was sadly aware, however, that to anyone else, it would look like a camera malfunction.

The third photo, however . . .

Poppy stared at it for a long time, torn between excitement and irritation.

The photo had captured a hand. A tiny hand. It looked, in fact, like a baby's hand.

Or it would have, that is, if it hadn't been making a rude gesture that no baby would know.

Poppy glared at the photo and gritted her teeth. It was very rude gesture indeed.

"Poppy?" Mrs. Malone asked. "Are you sure you're all right?"

Poppy blinked. She looked at her mother's concerned face. For just a second, she considered telling her everything—

Then the doorbell rang. Rolly came stampeding from the kitchen into the living room. He collided with Will, who had jumped up from the couch. They fell to the floor, knocking over a small table on the way and leaving the field open for Franny to step over them both and open the door. Only Poppy stayed put. She was checking one of the thermal-imaging cameras, which seemed to her to need some recalibrating.

"Honestly, I don't know why you children have

to fight each other to answer the door," said Mrs. Malone, righting the table. "Just because one time we happened to get a little present in the mail . . ."

In fact, Mr. Malone had once received an unexpected gift of three thousand dollars from a former client who was convinced that his farm was overrun with zombies who took a certain glee in letting his cows loose on moonless nights. (Mr. Malone had pinned his hopes on finding real zombies and was quite dashed to discover that one of the cows—clearly marked for leadership— had learned to open the gate by nudging the latch with her nose.)

The arrival of several thousand dollars in the mail was unprecedented, and it had made quite an impression on the Malone children. They never gave up hoping, with each mail delivery, that another windfall was about to arrive.

On this particular day, however, it was a special delivery box—battered and stained in a most promising way—that had arrived with a thump on the front porch.

The Malones squinted at the return label. The name and address had smeared into a large blot of blurry ink, but they could make out the last few letters of the sender's name—UITH. The stamps showed it had been mailed from Moldovia.

"It's from Oliver Asquith!" Mr. Malone exclaimed. "I didn't know he was still tracking that vampire cult through the Carpathian Mountains!"

"Oh yes, dear, remember he wrote to us," said Mrs. Malone. "He was about to give up but then Sam Oldham—you know, that odd young man who worked as his research assistant—well, he told Oliver he was going for a midnight stroll past an old churchyard, and the next thing Oliver knew, the police were knocking on his door and asking him to identify the body."

"That sort of thing always seems to happen to Oliver, doesn't it?" Mr. Malone said with a touch of satisfaction. He always cheered up when he heard about the problems of other researchers. "I'm surprised he can still get anyone to work with him."

"Oh, well, you know what graduate students

are like," said Mrs. Malone. "Anything for a job. And of course Oliver does do those TV specials, and you know how young people like to be in front of the camera."

Mr. Malone's smug expression disappeared. "Publicity hounds, the whole lot of them, and Oliver Asquith is the worst of the bunch. Those TV shows bring disrepute on our entire profession! I keep saying, they should be banned. We should put it to a vote with the entire membership of PSI—"

"All of whom want desperately to host their own show someday," said Mrs. Malone. "It would never pass, dear, and you know it."

Poppy carefully did not look at Will or Franny. They all knew that their father had spent years pitching his idea for a TV show to several cable networks. The show was to focus on the weekly adventures of a family of paranormal investigators (starring Mr. Malone, of course, with his wife and children in decidedly secondary roles).

"I still don't know why they won't pick up my show," said Mr. Malone, for perhaps the hundredth time. "No vision, that's their problem! Complete and utter shortsightedness!"

"Of course you're right, dear," said Mrs. Malone. "I'm sure it doesn't help that Oliver's show is so very popular, though. Perhaps the networks don't feel they need two shows about paranormal investigators . . . ?"

"That's ridiculous!" Mr. Malone glowered at her. "My show would easily get ten times as many viewers as Oliver's."

"But Professor Asquith is a lot younger than you, Dad, and really good-looking," said Franny. "His website gets millions of hits—"

"And how would you know that?" asked her father. "I seem to remember expressly forbidding you children from reading anything about that charlatan—"

"You said we couldn't read any of his books," said Franny. (Oliver Asquith had also published two books about his travels around the world in search of the paranormal, which had, most regrettably, sold hundreds of thousands of copies.)

"You didn't say we couldn't read his website."

"Before I end my days on this earth, I hope to teach my children the difference between the letter of the law and the spirit of the law," said Mr. Malone to no one in particular. "In the meantime, let me be perfectly clear: None of you are allowed to watch any TV shows or read any books, articles, or websites that feature the work of Oliver Asquith. His methods are completely unsound."

"He is rather unconventional," said Mrs. Malone, "but his heart is in the right place, and he always sends such *interesting* gifts."

"Right," muttered Will. "Like the Peruvian sorcerer's powder that gave all of us that interesting rash."

"Maybe we should stand back while Dad opens it," Poppy suggested, giving the box a testing nudge with her toe.

"Maybe we should go out for ice cream and come back when it's safe," said Franny.

"Faint hearts!" said Mr. Malone. He pulled off the envelope that had been taped to the box and handed it to his wife, then took out his pocketknife and got to work opening the box itself.

Mrs. Malone put on her reading glasses, opened the envelope, and peered at the crumpled note inside.

"Oliver says he hopes we're settling into our new home and will accept this housewarming gift. How sweet," she said. "Hmm . . . it seems he's given up on vampires . . . given up on Moldovia, too. . . . oh dear, he says he had to leave in the dead of night; I wonder what *that* was all about. . . . Now he's in Slovakia, which he thinks will offer much better prospects for his next phase of research. . . ."

For all his bravado, Mr. Malone had taken his time slitting the box open. He gingerly pulled back the top and removed a layer of packing material to reveal six long wooden sticks nestled in a mass of shredded paper.

"Hey, maybe those are special wooden stakes he used to take out a Moldovian vampire," Will said, getting interested in spite of himself. "Maybe they have bloodstains on them!"

Mrs. Malone pulled one of the sticks out of the box, and they saw that it had a forked end. "A dowsing rod!" she said with delight. "How nice of Oliver to remember!"

Poppy knew that people used dowsing rods to find underground water or buried pipes; when the end of the rod dipped toward the ground, you knew where to dig. She took a rod out of the box and pointed it experimentally at a rosebush. "Remember what?"

"About the ley lines that converge here," said Mr. Malone. He held the forked end of a rod in his hands and pointed the end in the direction of the front sidewalk. "Have I told you about my latest theory . . . ?"

"Yes!" his family answered in chorus, but it was no use. Mr. Malone ignored them and launched himself once more into the lecture that they had been hearing, in various forms, ever since he and Mrs. Malone had won the foundation grant.

Many people, it seemed, believed in ley lines—lines of magnetic force that circled the globe. Ley lines were often associated with mysteries such as Stonehenge in England or the Nazca Lines in Peru. Mr. Malone had followed these reports with keen interest for a number of years and had begun tracking the lines on his computer in his spare time.

It was his astonishing discovery that a number of ley lines all converged beneath Austin, Texas, that had led to his theory. If one ley line was powerful, he reasoned, the spot where two lines crossed (Mr. Malone named this "the node of energy") would be doubly so. When he discovered that no fewer than ten lines ran underneath Austin, he had been beside himself with excitement. This, he declared, meant that that paranormal forces would be stronger in Austin than anywhere in the world.

"UFOs must be attracted to the area like moths to a flame!" he had told his family. "The place will be swarming with ghosts; we'll have our pick of hauntings to investigate. I wouldn't be surprised if there's a whole herd of Bigfoot—"

"Bigfeet?" Will had suggested under his breath.

"—roaming the hills. Vampires, werewolves, mysterious lights in the night sky, they'll all be there for the taking."

Poppy thought that he had sounded a bit like the American pioneers who had decided to travel west to a bountiful Promised Land. Apparently, his enthusiasm had been contagious. He had included his theory in the grant application and later learned that it was the reason Mr. and Mrs. Malone had won.

Now he looked at the box of dowsing rods with gleaming eyes. "Six dowsing rods," he noted. "One for each of us. We could take them on a test run right now." He smiled and swung the dowsing rod in his hand encouragingly. "Well, what do you say? Who's with me?"

Disappointingly, no one was.

One by one and murmuring vague excuses, Franny, Will, Poppy, and Rolly wandered away.

"They're just tired, dear," Mrs. Malone said. "There will be plenty of time to test out the dowsing rods later."

As Poppy climbed the stairs, she could hear her mother reading the end of the letter.

"Oliver says he bought the dowsing rods from a well-known Slovakian witch," Mrs. Malone said. "Well, I do hope he offered a fair price; you know how witches like to curse things when they feel they've been underpaid. . . ."

Chapter
SEVEN

The knocking began just after midnight.

First it was just one rap, then two. Each one was soft, almost tentative, and they came five or ten minutes apart. It was easy for Poppy to ignore.

Then the rapping got louder and bolder, and seemed to be coming from every corner of the house. Three brisk knocks would come under the floorboards, then five even more rapid raps would sound from inside the closet. A brief pause, then a series of bangs would come from the ceiling, as if someone were pounding the floor above her room with the end of a broom handle.

After a particularly loud tattoo, Poppy jumped out of bed and went into the hall, where she found the rest of her family standing in their pajamas. Will was blinking sleepily, and Franny looked cross. Mr. Malone's thin brown hair was sticking up in little tufts and there was a pillow crease on his cheek, but he looked quite bouncy and cheerful, while Mrs. Malone, wearing a pink chenille bathrobe and slippers, positively fizzed with energy.

"Did you all hear that?" Mr. Malone asked.

"We'd have to be deaf not to hear it," said Franny. "It sounds like a drum and bugle corps invaded our house. Only without the bugles."

"Isn't it thrilling?" cried Mrs. Malone. "Aren't you excited?"

"No and no," said Will. His eyelids were drooping, and he swayed on his feet. "I'm sleepy."

"So what else is new?" said Franny under her breath.

Will managed to open his eyes long enough to give her a scornful look. "I know it seems strange that I'm tired," he said sarcastically, "especially since it's the middle of the night."

"Will you children stop talking for two seconds

and listen?" snapped Mr. Malone. "Here we are, face-to-face with an actual paranormal experience, and all you can do is think about going back to bed."

They all rolled their eyes, but they stopped talking and listened.

The silence lasted for exactly thirty-six seconds. (Poppy, who often forgot to take off her watch before bed, was timing it.) This was long enough for all of them—except Mr. and Mrs. Malone, of course—to begin to hope that the noise was over, for the rest of the night, at least. Will even yawned and began drifting back toward his bedroom.

Then the stillness was broken by a sudden series of bangs. Franny jumped. Will groaned and leaned heavily against the wall.

Mr. and Mrs. Malone beamed.

"It's the Dark Presence," said Mr. Malone. "Your mother spotted it immediately, and she was absolutely right."

"Well, it was fairly obvious to anyone with any degree of field experience," Mrs. Malone murmured, smiling modestly at the floor.

"Did you hear the force of those bangs, Lucille?" Mr. Malone asked. "The scale of the activity is unbelievable."

"It's probably just a tree branch hitting the window," said Poppy.

"Or pipes banging," said Franny.

"Or the house settling," Will added, yawning hugely.

Their father gave them a disillusioned look. "I don't know where we went wrong raising you children," he said. "Your mother and I certainly tried our best, but—"

He was interrupted by a sudden sharp bang.

The Malones all jumped.

"Aha!" Mr. Malone said triumphantly. "And what do you think *that* was?"

"A loose shutter," said Poppy.

"There's no wind," said Mrs. Malone. "I'm getting the digital recorder."

"Wait a second," Poppy interrupted. "Where's Rolly?"

"I'm sure he's fast asleep," her mother said with a bit too much confidence.

"Fast asleep?" asked Franny. "With all this racket?"

"We'd better make sure," said Will. "It would be just like him to run around the house pounding on walls."

"Really, Will," said Mrs. Malone. "Why in the world would he do that?"

"Why does Rolly do anything?" asked Poppy. To which no one had an answer.

But when they checked his room, they found Rolly asleep, although his pillow was on the floor and his quilt was bunched at the foot of his bed. (Rolly tended to make messes, even in his dreams.)

"He looks just like a little angel, doesn't he?" Mrs. Malone whispered with a fond smile.

This comment was greeted with silence from the rest of the family.

"Wouldn't you love to know what he's dreaming about?" asked Mrs. Malone.

"World domination, probably," said Will under

his breath, while Poppy secretly pinched Rolly's toe to make sure he was really asleep.

Then they trooped back into the hall and stood in a little circle, staring at one another and listening to the raps, which had slowed down and were now coming every five minutes or so. In a way, that was worse, since the silences would lull them into thinking that the bombardment was over.

"Don't worry," said Poppy. "It's probably just mice."

She meant this to be consoling. After all, mice were normal. Anyone could have mice.

"Mice?" said Franny, standing on her tiptoes and peering nervously at the floorboards. "Honestly! As if ghosts weren't bad enough . . ."

Another series of brisk taps echoed through the hall.

"Mice with little fists?" asked Mr. Malone. He knelt down and tried to press his ear to the baseboard. "I think I can hear something moving between the walls—"

"That's it," Franny snapped. "I'm going back to

bed." With that, she flounced back into her bed-room and slammed the door.

"I'm going to bed, too," said Will. "I may not be able to sleep, but at least I'll be horizontal."

He trudged off, yawning.

"I don't know how we raised two children with so little vim or vigor," Mr. Malone commented as he watched Franny and Will stagger back to bed. "When I was their age, I stayed up all night just on the off chance that I might spot the Moth Man of New Jersey! I can still go without sleep for days without even drinking one cup of coffee!"

"It's a gift, dear," Mrs. Malone said sooth-ingly. "We can't expect to pass it down to all of our children."

Mr. Malone sighed, but nodded. "At least we have Poppy," he said. "You wouldn't abandon a budding investigation just to get a few extra winks of sleep, would you, Poppy?"

Poppy, blinking, managed to cover her yawn just in time.

* * *

Still stifling her yawns, Poppy went downstairs, got a flashlight from the kitchen cupboard, and tiptoed outside. A full moon floated in the sky, so she didn't turn on the flashlight. She stood in the driveway, feeling the warm night air against her skin and letting her eyes adjust to the dark.

Something moved in the shadows. Poppy held her breath and listened.

She heard leaves rustle, but that could have been a raccoon or possum. She heard what sounded like a whisper, but that could have been a snake slipping through the grass.

And then she heard a snicker.

It was quickly muffled, but she knew she had heard it.

Quickly, she turned on the flashlight and swept the yard with its beam. She lit up a bush, then a tree, then the ladder still leaning against the side of the house. Nothing unusual. Nothing strange. Nothing remotely goblinish.

Then she heard the rattle of a window being opened, and she tilted her head back to see Rolly, framed in a square of light on the second floor.

"Rolly?" she called up to him. "What are you doing?"

Very slowly, as if he were dreaming, he turned to look at her.

"Nothing," he said slowly. His voice sounded sleepy.

"Close the window and go to bed," she said. She wondered if he was sleepwalking. Poppy had heard about people who did all kinds of crazy things while still asleep, like driving cars or turning on ovens or starting fires; the thought that Rolly could potentially have eight additional hours each day to create chaos was a chilling one indeed.

But after a long moment, he disappeared from the window. A few seconds later, his light switched off.

When Poppy went back inside the house, she found her parents in the living room, trying to encourage each other. They were disappointed that the knocking seemed to have ended for the night.

"This was probably just the first salvo," said

Mr. Malone. "In my experience, a Dark Presence doesn't give up after one try."

"You're right, of course," said Mrs. Malone. "We should go to bed and try to get a good night's sleep so that we can be rested for Whatever Comes. I'm sure we'll have to deal with manifestations that are far, far worse before long!"

Although her mother tried to make her words sound ominous, Poppy could tell she was disheartened.

But as it turned out, Mrs. Malone was more right than she could have imagined.

Chapter
EIGHT

"**I** foresee disaster," muttered Will.

He was sitting at the breakfast table, watching as Mrs. Malone mixed pancake batter with short, irritated strokes.

"Stop trying to pretend you're psychic," Poppy said grumpily. "We *all* foresee disaster."

Mrs. Malone glanced over her shoulder. There was a streak of flour on her forehead and a smear of butter on her glasses. She looked hot and anxious. "What are you two whispering about?" she asked.

They turned innocent faces in her direction. "Nothing," they chorused.

"I keep telling you children, I need to concentrate." Mrs. Malone was holding a cookbook in one hand and a spoon in the other. "And I can't concentrate with my own family muttering behind my back like a gang of mafioso."

Poppy and Will made expressive faces at each other, but they stopped talking. Nerves were frayed to the breaking point in the Malone household where, for the past three days, it seemed that everything that *could* go wrong *did* go wrong.

If something could spill, it did: Mr. Malone left a can of paint on the porch railing and went inside for some iced tea, only to return and find the can tipped over and paint dripping down the front steps. Mrs. Malone walked into the kitchen one day to discover piles of sugar drifting across the pantry shelves. Will tidily bagged the week's garbage and put it in cans by the curb, only to find the contents strewn across the driveway the next morning.

All of that could be explained away, of course. A paint can balanced on a porch railing is likely to fall. The pantry had mice. Raccoons were famous for getting into garbage cans.

But there were other little problems. No one could

find anything they needed when they needed it. Mr. Malone misplaced his keys several times a day and his solar charger—the one he always carried when his investigations took him to remote locations—was nowhere to be found. Mrs. Malone had to drive to the store three times in three days to buy more batteries to replace the ones that had mysteriously disappeared in the night. Anything that came in a pair, such as socks, sneakers, or earrings, was reduced to a single. Franny constantly flew around the house in a rage, trying to find her favorite lipstick, her favorite necklace, her favorite headband.

Still, they all knew what it was like settling into a new house. It takes a while to get your bearings, to develop little habits like always putting your keys in the same place. And so much stuff was being moved here and there as the Malones kept unpacking and settling in—it was a wonder, Mrs. Malone said, that they could find their own beds at night.

Mrs. Malone was, however, annoyed by how forgetful everyone else in the family had become. "Really," she said one afternoon, "you are all becoming most irresponsible. I came down this morning to find the back door wide open. Yesterday, I walked into a completely empty living room and found that someone had left the TV and all the lights on. And whoever left the faucet running upstairs—"

"Owes me money," interrupted Mr. Malone. "The water bill this month is going to be enormous. I should cut everyone's allowance until it's paid off! If I were any kind of father, I would!"

The Malone children kept very still and silent. They usually entered into a spirited and generally friendly debate when Mr. Malone uttered such threats, knowing that they were rarely serious, but he had just stirred two spoonfuls of sugar into his coffee only to discover that the sugar bowl was filled with salt. It didn't seem like a good time to risk making a wrong move.

And there were other annoyances.

The fuses blew three times in one afternoon, plunging the house into darkness; the smoke alarm went off randomly throughout the day; and lightbulbs kept popping at inconvenient times. All this, said Mr. Malone, was undoubtedly the fault of the house's ancient electrical wiring. He then started making rough calculations about how much it would cost to rewire the entire house, which only deepened his gloom.

Will's hard drive went down, wiping out all his songs. A ballpoint pen leaked ink all over Poppy's logbook (ruining the three goblin photos she had carefully pasted inside, which she couldn't believe was a coincidence). A bottle of Franny's favorite gardenia perfume fell to the floor and broke, filling the bathroom with a powerful scent that lingered for days.

The car tires went flat. The mailbox was pushed over. Nobody's computer passwords worked.

And every night, the knocking started shortly after midnight and didn't let up until dawn.

After three days, Franny and Will were in open revolt, demanding that the family decamp to a hotel until the Dark Presence could be exorcised. Poppy found herself jumping at loud noises and thinking that she had just seen something out of the corner of her eye. Even Mr. and Mrs. Malone were beginning to look pensive.

That very morning, after yet another sleepless night, Mr. Malone had decided to take a hot shower to wake up. Halfway through, the hot water went off and he was abruptly drenched with an icy downpour.

His screams of outrage drowned out Franny's calls for help. She had arisen, bleary eyed and grumpy, only to have the doorknob come off when she tried to open her bedroom door, trapping her inside. After waiting for fifteen minutes with no sign of rescue, she had been forced to climb out her window and down a drainpipe.

Will woke up to find that all the strings on his electric guitar had snapped during the night.

Poppy discovered that the wastebasket in her room had tipped over, spilling crumpled papers and pencil shavings across the floor.

Mrs. Malone staggered down to the kitchen to make a pot of coffee and found coffee grounds scattered on the windowsills.

So now, as they sat around the kitchen table

waiting for breakfast, only Rolly seemed happy, humming an off-key tune and kicking the legs of his chair.

"Rolly, *please*." Mrs. Malone pushed a few damp strands of hair off her forehead, watching closely as a pat of butter melted in the pan. "Stop making that noise, darling, at least until I finish this first batch. You're making me nervous."

"Mom." Franny had her head propped on one hand so that her hair fell into her face. With a great effort, she managed to flip a strand back and roll her eyes. "Let's just have cereal. For heaven's sake. I don't even like pancakes."

"The last few days have been very difficult. A nice hot breakfast will give us the strength and resolve we will need to prevail over whatever supernatural forces we will be asked to face in the weeks ahead." She looked over her glasses at her children. "Cereal does not set the right tone at all."

"Whatever." Franny let her hair fall back over her face and put her head back down on her arms.

As Mrs. Malone poured batter into the pan, Mr.

Malone bounded into the kitchen, brimming with good cheer. "Good morning, everyone! Ah, pancakes, wonderful! Just the thing to give us a little extra pep today!"

"What's put you in such a good mood?" asked Will suspiciously. "Did the hot water come back on?"

"No, but I've risen above it," said Mr. Malone. "After all, one's true character is revealed by how one faces adversity. It's true that we've all had our challenges recently—"

"Challenges!" Franny cried. "I had to climb down the drainpipe! In my pajamas! In broad daylight!"

Will said, "My hard drive—"

Poppy added, "My notebooks—"

"Get dressed before you climb out your window," their father said briskly. "Back up your hard drive. Put your pens away."

He poured a glass of orange juice with the air of someone who was suffering bravely and in silence. Then he smiled benevolently at his children and said, "While I admit that it's trying to experience incidents of a supernatural and perhaps even malevolent nature, we must remain strong and resolute. If this case follows the usual course, we should have slime on the walls and howling in the attic within the week."

Mrs. Malone turned away from the stove. "Oh, I hope this doesn't go as far as slime," she said. "Not that I wouldn't like to replace the wallpaper in the living room, but it's always so hard to get the smell out."

"We must be strong," said Mr. Malone. "Slime might very well be the least of it—watch the stove!"

Mrs. Malone whipped around to find a column of smoke rising toward the ceiling and the charred remains of her pancakes smoldering in the pan. "Oh, drat, drat, and double drat!"

"The Dark Presence makes himself known once again," said Will under his breath.

"As soon as I get my computer fixed," said Mr. Malone, "I'm going online to do more research—Rolly, stop that right now!"

"What?" Rolly looked up, his black eyes round with surprise.

No one had noticed him methodically pouring syrup in an intricate pattern on his plate. Or, when he decided that his plate was too limiting a canvas, pouring syrup on the tablecloth.

"I can't believe it," said Franny, suddenly realizing that strands of her hair had trailed into the syrup. "Now I have to go and wash my hair *again*!"

"We don't have time for that right now," said Mrs. Malone, looking at the pan, which was again smoking in an ominous manner. "Will, help Rolly wash his face. And everyone stand back while I flip these over—"

"I don't know why you always make such a big deal about flipping pancakes," Will said, grabbing a dish towel.

"Pancakes are trickier than they look," said Mrs. Malone.

"It's perfectly simple," said Will, turning on the faucet. "You just need to put some wrist action into it—"

The water shot up at an angle, hitting him in the face.

Will yelped and jumped back, dripping and outraged. His foot skidded on the floor, causing him to crash into the table just as Mrs. Malone said indignantly, "I put plenty of wrist action into my pancakes, thank you very much."

"Watch out!" Poppy sprang to her feet and reached for the pitcher, but she was too late. Milk flowed across the table and onto the floor.

"Ye gods and little fishes!" yelled Mr. Malone, who tried to jump out of the milk's way and bumped into Mrs. Malone just as she was demonstrating her wrist action.

She stared at him with exasperation. "Really, Emerson! I had everything perfectly under control until you decided to go leaping about the kitchen."

With an annoyed glance at the ceiling, she poured more batter into the pan. "Honestly. Sometimes I think that a whole houseful of poltergeists would be less trouble than this family. . . ."

Chapter NINE

"How crazy do you think our parents are?" asked Will, who was stretched out on the porch swing, watching Mr. and Mrs. Malone through half-closed eyes. They were wandering back and forth on the lawn, holding their dowsing rods in front of them. "I mean on a scale of one to ten?"

"Ten being the craziest?" Franny asked. She was sitting on the porch railing, her head back against a column, her eyes closed against the afternoon sun. She opened one eye just long enough to see Will nod, then she closed it again. "I'd say they rate a twenty-three at least. Twenty-five if you count the way they're dressed."

Mrs. Malone wore shorts, a T-shirt, sneakers,

and an enormous straw hat draped with a veil. The hat had belonged to the subject of Mrs. Malone's very first haunting case: a fashionable young Victorian woman who had caught a fatal chill after insisting on wearing a taffeta gown to a winter dance. Mr. Malone was dressed in a neon orange Hawaiian shirt, khaki shorts, and a pith helmet he'd brought back from a South American trip to research werewolf cults.

Poppy watched as her mother's dowsing rod suddenly pointed down at the ground, then began quivering. Mrs. Malone zigzagged across the lawn as the rod seemingly pulled her along. She looked as if she had a large, ill-trained, and invisible dog on a leash.

"I can't believe they're still at it," Poppy said. "You'd think they'd get tired. You'd think they'd get *hot*."

Will yawned. "They keep saying they've seen something out of the corner of their eyes . . . *wooooo*!" He mustered up enough energy to flutter his fingers mysteriously in the air before letting his hand drop to his side.

113

"So much for starting over in a new town where nobody knows us," Franny said bitterly. "So much for trying to at least *pretend* that we're normal."

"Maybe people will think they're doing lawn work," said Poppy. "They could be measuring space for a flowerbed."

"Or for a grave," said Will in a hollow voice.

"Stop it, Will." Franny took a barrette out of her hair and threw it at him, which was a sign of extreme displeasure. Under normal circumstances, she jealously guarded all her accessories and was known to break down in hysterics if she lost an earring or favorite ponytail holder. "It's bad enough that I can't go to sleep at night without wondering who might have died a gruesome death in my bedroom."

"Franny! Will! Poppy!" Their father seemed to catch sight of them for the first time. "Grab a dowsing rod and come help us!"

Franny looked appalled at this suggestion. She quickly slipped back inside the house, muttering something about making lemonade.

Will quickly closed his eyes and began massaging his temples, as if he were trying to tune into a sudden vision.

Poppy simply called out, "In a minute, Dad!" She kept rocking and thinking about goblins as she watched her parents stagger around the lawn. Last night, she had snuck downstairs and dug through a half-dozen unpacked boxes of books before finding the one she wanted. It was a book called *The Little People: A Comprehensive History of Hobgoblins, Pixies, Brownies, and Sprites*. She had been reading bits and pieces in secret whenever she could snatch a few moments alone. Now, she opened the book again—she had covered it with the dust jacket from an astronomy book—and picked up where she had left off.

"The people there are much like ourselves, only they are very small and roguish," she read. "They enjoy making mischief, but can be placated through small gifts. A Scottish minister in the seventeenth century noted in a pamphlet on this subject that people in his parish often left bowls of milk or freshly baked bread by their back door as a peace offering. Other observers have noted that the little people are particularly fond of small, shiny objects such as jewelry and silver teaspoons."

Poppy curled her lip at that. As if she would stoop as low as bribery!

She kept reading, but gradually the heat, the steady creak of the porch swing, and a large lunch began to take their toll. Poppy's eyes began to close. . . .

Then something rustled in the bushes next to the porch.

Her eyes snapped open. Very slowly, she turned her head in the direction of the noise. There was an overgrown, untidy bush between the porch railing and the side of the house. There was only one flower on the bush, a pink one the size of a saucer. It was quivering in the still air as if something— or someone—was moving stealthily through the foliage.

Of course, it could be a cat, Poppy thought, even as she eased herself out of the rocker and moved, ever so slowly, over to the railing. Or maybe a squirrel . . .

She had taken only four steps when she spotted the goblin. It was not the one she had seen before; she was sure of it. For one thing, this goblin was even smaller, smaller than a hollyhock (she could tell, because he happened to be standing right next to a hollyhock plant). He also seemed less self-assured. He was fidgeting a bit, rocking from one foot to the other and nervously rubbing his fingers together. In fact, that was the only reason she had noticed him. He was wearing green clothing that blended into the leaves; if he had stayed perfectly still, she probably wouldn't have spotted him.

He squinted at her parents with a look of extreme concentration. He was so focused, in fact, that Poppy thought she might have a chance to creep up on him without him noticing, and maybe even grab him.

Holding her breath, she slid one foot forward, then another. As she inched her way slowly to the edge of the porch, she saw him reach toward a faucet on the side of the house. . . .

The next thing she knew, all of the lawn sprinklers were turned on full force.

"Aaggh!" Mrs. Malone shrieked, and shot into the air as a jet of water hit her in the back of her knees.

Mr. Malone turned around and got a blast of cold water in the face. He leaped back, slipped, and began windmilling his arms wildly to regain his balance.

It didn't work. He crashed to the ground.

Poppy was distracted for only a moment, but it was long enough. When she looked back, the goblin was gone.

Rolly trotted around the corner of the house just as Mrs. Malone helped her husband get to his feet.

"Rolly!" Mr. Malone limped over to the porch, supported by his wife. He had one hand pressed to his back and was bending over in a funny way. "What in the world do you think you're doing?"

Rolly looked blankly at his father. "But I didn't—"

"Do it," his father finished for him. "Of course you didn't."

"Now, Emerson, there's no reason to be sarcastic," said Mrs. Malone automatically, although even she gave her youngest a reproving look. "Rolly, dear, you really shouldn't play with the sprinklers."

Rolly's lower lip jutted out. "But I *didn't*—"

"No? Then how did you get all that mud on your clothes?" Mr. Malone exclaimed, just like a prosecuting attorney springing a trap.

"What?" Rolly looked down at himself. His sneakers were caked with mud. His shorts looked as though he'd spent a fair amount of time sitting in a puddle. And his shirt was streaked with dirt where he had obviously wiped his hands. He looked back up at his father, puzzled. "I don't know."

"No, no, of course you don't," said Mr. Malone as he began hobbling gingerly toward the front door. "Amazing how baseballs crash through windows and worms appear in soup and sprinklers turn on all by themselves and you never know anything about it. It's always a complete mystery to you, isn't it?"

"Really, Emerson, you're going to hurt poor Rolly's feelings," Mrs. Malone protested.

"You know, Lucille, we really should try hypnotic regression to see if he's lived past lives," Mr. Malone went on, ignoring her as he stiffly climbed the porch steps. "I wouldn't be surprised to find out that he was lurking about at the fall of Jericho and the destruction of Atlantis! I'll bet he was on hand when the Library at Alexandria burned and barbarians stormed the gates of Rome! And I am furthermore quite sure that if some poor soul managed to rise up from the ruins to ask what had just happened"—having reached the porch, he turned to glare down at Rolly—"I'm sure he said, *'I don't know!'*"

They all stood silent for a moment. Even Rolly looked impressed by this impassioned speech.

"But Dad," Poppy began, thinking of a small goblin hand reaching for the faucet.

He stopped mid-hobble and glared over his shoulder. *"What?"*

She hesitated. "Let me open the door for you."

Thanks to Rolly, the Malones knew many interesting things. They knew that an inflatable swimming pool holds enough water to flood a neighbor's prize-winning vegetable garden, that a ceiling fan can hit a baseball hard enough to break a double-paned window, and that no amount of air freshener can ever completely mask the odor after a small pan of ammonia is left on top of a radiator. They had learned that microwaving plastic army men causes a choking smell that can make grown men cry; that adding an entire box of detergent to the washing machine creates enough suds to fill a laundry room two feet deep; and that a dead mouse can be stored in a freezer for up to five months. Although many people know that magnifying glasses can be used to set twigs and leaves on fire, the Malones could also reel off the response times of fire departments in six cities.

Considering the results of Rolly's other experiments, the Incident of the Water Sprinklers was a minor escapade. Nonetheless, he was in disgrace, although it wasn't clear whether he knew it or, if he did, whether he cared.

Mrs. Malone insisted that Rolly stay within eyesight at all times, and Mr. Malone clutched his back and shot him dark looks whenever they crossed paths, but Rolly was absorbed with his own thoughts and barely noticed. He didn't seem to notice anything, in fact, until one morning, shortly after breakfast, when he trotted into the kitchen with larceny on his mind.

He was going in search of teeth-achingly sweet chocolates called Choc-O-Bombs. Rolly was abnormally fond of this candy and was, in fact, the only Malone who would eat them. (The rest of the family used to enjoy Choc-O-Bombs as well. Then Will pointed out that the gooey cherry-vanilla filling looked like brains and that eating one made him feel like a zombie biting into a human skull. That had put everyone except Rolly off Choc-O-Bombs for life.)

Mrs. Malone hid these treats high up in the pantry, but that presented no problem to Rolly, who had long ago learned the art of climbing pantry shelves. He had also learned to hide the distinctive red-and-gold Choc-O-Bomb wrappers in places where no one would find them. Any spot behind a curtain or under a couch worked well, since no one in the family dusted or swept, except on the rare occasions when Mrs. Malone came out of her preoccupied daze and declared that unless Something Was Done, their house would be condemned by the department of health.

But instead of the nice, empty kitchen Rolly expected that morning, he found his older brother and sisters busily packing lunch bags with sandwiches, bags of chips, and (after some firm encouragement from their mother) apples and oranges.

"What are you doing?" Rolly asked.

"Nothing," Will said in a voice so innocent that he ended up sounding decidedly shifty.

"You are," said Rolly. "You're going somewhere. You're going somewhere without me."

"No, we're not," said Franny.

"I want to go, too."

"You can't," said Poppy, slathering peanut butter on a piece of bread. "We're going to explore the woods. You're too little. You wouldn't like it."

"Yes, I would!" Rolly insisted.

"You really wouldn't," Poppy said in a reasonable tone. "We're going on a long, long, *long* walk. You'll get tired."

"No, I won't."

"You always get tired," said Will. "And then we always have to come home early."

"Or you get in trouble, which means we get in trouble because we weren't watching you," Franny added.

"Then stay here," said Rolly. "Play with me."

"Later," said Poppy. "When we get back."

Rolly sat down, sliding in his chair until only his eyes could be seen above the tabletop. "You always say you'll play with me later and then you don't."

Poppy glanced toward the window. Outside,

the bright day beckoned with a high blue sky, sunshine, and, just on the other side of the road, the green mysterious darkness of the woods. "We will, really we will," she said, her mind already leaping ahead to what adventures the day might hold. "Promise."

It was late afternoon when Poppy began to have the uncomfortable feeling that they were being watched. They had spent hours in the woods, following faint trails through tangled undergrowth, searching for secret hiding spaces, and imagining what it would have been like to live there two hundred years ago.

By lunchtime, Franny had fallen into a small creek, Will had found a triangular rock that was almost certainly an arrowhead, and Poppy had stumbled upon a wasps' nest (luckily abandoned). They had spotted tracks in the mud and argued amiably for some time about what animal they belonged to. They had seen a snake slither across their path and disappear into the long grass, and had felt the shiver up the spine that even a harmless garter snake could cause. They had discovered a patch of blackberry bushes, so heavy with fruit that they all agreed that they were probably the first people ever to have discovered it. They picked blackberries, feeling like pioneers foraging on the land, eating them until their lips had turned purple.

This took some time, and they found that the blackberries had taken the edge off their hunger, so it was late in the afternoon before they were ready to eat the lunches they'd prepared. They found a log to sit on and unwrapped their sandwiches. For a few moments, the only sounds were the leaves stirring in the wind, occasional bursts of birdsong, and the constant buzz of insects. Poppy realized that even the most ordinary food, like a peanut butter sandwich, tasted more interesting when eaten outside, a discovery that she made every summer with the same feeling of surprise.

Once she'd finished eating, she sat for a few minutes listening to water trickling over rocks in the creek, her mind drifting pleasantly from one non-thought to another. Then, gradually, she became aware of a rustling in the bushes behind her. She opened her eyes and sat up a little straighter, willing herself not to turn around and look.

The rustling stopped. Poppy froze and listened as hard as she could, but she didn't hear another sound. Still, the back of her neck was prickling as if someone were staring at her.

Slowly, she stood up, almost holding her breath. The sensation of being watched grew stronger.

She turned around quickly, scanning the bushes. Nothing.

She gave herself a slight shake. It's a normal day in a normal park, she reminded herself. Stop imagining things. Do something normal.

"Hey, Will." She walked over to where he was lying on the grass, one arm flung over his face. "Let's walk back to the creek and look for more animal tracks."

"Taking a nap," he muttered. "Later."

Poppy rolled her eyes, but she knew better than

to interrupt him when he was dozing off. "What about you, Franny?"

But Franny was sitting in a patch of sunlight, tilting her face toward the sky with her eyes closed. "Not now," she said. "I'm working on my fresh, natural glow."

"Your what?"

Franny sighed a deep sigh, as if the bounds of her patience were being stretched beyond endurance. "I read about it in a magazine. Ten minutes of natural light a day will give your face a fresh, natural glow." She opened one eye to give Poppy a defiant look. "It's been scientifically proven."

Poppy doubted that, but decided not to argue. Fine, she thought. If they want to just sit around, let them. I'm going to . . . She looked around and saw a large, gnarled oak tree with thick, low branches.

Ten minutes later, she was perched an exhilarating distance above the ground, with a panoramic view of the world and all its inhabitants.

She settled her back against the trunk and looked around. Her view of the world, as it turned out, was mostly trees, and the only inhabitants appeared to be squirrels running up and down tree trunks and the occasional bird winging by. Far below to her right, she could see Will napping and Franny sunning herself. And far below to her left, she could see the trail wending its way toward home and a small, humanlike figure marching in her direction. . . .

Poppy sat up suddenly, almost lost her balance, and grabbed the trunk to steady herself. She looked again, and saw that it was Rolly. He was trotting along, his head swiveling from one side of the trail to the other. He was searching for something. Or someone. Three someones, in fact.

Quickly, she climbed down the tree. They should have realized that Rolly would give their mother the slip and follow them, she thought. They should have been smart enough to cover their tracks. Now it was too late.

"I just saw Rolly coming this way," she told Will and Franny. "He's looking for us."

Franny opened her eyes, blinking in the

sunlight. *"Honestly."* Frowning, she took a ponytail holder from her pocket and pulled her hair back in one swift motion. "I don't know anyone else who has a little brother who is such a *pest*."

"He just wants to hang out with us," said Poppy, trying to be fair. "You can't blame him for that, not really—"

"I can and I do!" Franny cried. "We've told him a million times to stay at home and not bother us. For heaven's sake. He's practically a baby. Why doesn't he find some friends his own age to play with?"

This suggestion was ignored.

"He'll probably want to play hide-and-seek," Will said gloomily. "And we'll probably all end up with poison ivy. Everyone except Rolly, of course." He kicked at a stone. "Has anyone else noticed how complicated our lives got after Rolly was born?"

Franny's face brightened. "I know!" she said. "Why don't we hide so that he has to look for us? Maybe he'll get tired of looking and go home."

"I don't know," said Poppy slowly. "What if he gets scared?"

"Rolly? Scared?" scoffed Will. "Anyway, he's always hiding from *us*. It's only fair to turn the tables for once."

Poppy hesitated, but then she heard a low, tuneless humming. It was the sound Rolly made when he was completely focused on the task at hand.

"He's just around the bend," said Will. "Quick! Hide!"

There was such urgency in Will's voice that Poppy, without thinking, ran toward the creek. She had noticed a large flat rock covered with moss when they had been looking for animal tracks earlier. It was shielded by a tree and several large bushes. It was a perfect hiding place.

She pushed through the bushes and sat on the rock, trying to quiet her breathing so that she could hear Rolly's approach. She heard crackling and rustling as Will and Franny found their own hiding places. And then all was quiet.

Poppy sat as still as possible, her heart rate

gradually slowing down to normal. After a minute or two, Rolly's humming became louder. By peeking through the bushes, she could just catch a glimpse of him as he walked by on the trail.

Suddenly, he stopped, as if he'd heard something. He turned in a circle, slowly, peering intensely at the undergrowth. She had the strange feeling that he could see through the bushes and the tree trunk and that he was looking right at her. . . .

Her stomach clenched. She had always hated playing hide-and-seek when she was little; trying to avoid discovery made her so nervous that sometimes she would jump up just to end the game.

But then Rolly glanced away, as if something else had caught his attention. After a moment, he kept going down the trail. Poppy let out a sigh of relief, only then realizing that she'd been holding her breath.

She glanced at her watch. It was getting late. They should go home for supper soon. She'd give Rolly five minutes, and then she'd go after him. . . .

* * *

But ten minutes later, there was still no sign of Rolly. Poppy had stood up, dusted off the seat of her shorts, and walked down the trail without the slightest sense of foreboding. Rolly hadn't been walking fast; plus, his legs were short. It had only been ten minutes. She knew he couldn't have gotten far.

As she walked farther and farther, however, she started to get worried.

He'll be around the next bend, she told herself. Then she'd follow the curve, only to find the trail ahead empty.

I'll bet he's sitting on a log up ahead, she thought. He's probably getting tired by now. . . .

But he wasn't.

When she looked at her watch and saw that she'd been searching for fifteen minutes, Poppy turned around and headed back down the trail, almost running. She hadn't gone far before she encountered Franny and Will.

"Where's Rolly?" Franny asked. "We should go. It's getting dark."

"I don't know where he is," said Poppy. "I saw him head in this direction. I was sitting by the creek when he walked past." She checked her watch again. "He couldn't have gotten very far, even if he was running, which he wasn't, but I can't find him."

"Maybe he turned around and headed home when he couldn't find us," Will suggested.

Poppy gave him an exasperated look. "Will. Don't you think I'd have seen him? He would have walked right past me."

"Do you think he'd leave the trail?" asked Franny. "If he did, he could be anywhere. . . ."

For a moment, no one said anything.

Then Franny added, "Mom and Dad are going to be really mad if it turns out we lost Rolly."

"He's not lost," Poppy snapped. "He never is. He must have realized we were hiding from him, and now he's hiding from us. He's just playing a trick on us. As usual."

"Okay, let's split up and look for him," said Will. "We'll meet back here in fifteen minutes. If anyone finds Rolly before that, yell. Okay?"

They all nodded, although Franny's nod was reluctant. Poppy headed off the trail toward the creek, for no real reason except that she thought Rolly might have been attracted by the sound of the water. She pushed through bushes and stepped over logs, stopping every minute or so to call Rolly's name. In the distance, she could hear Franny and Will crashing about and yelling for Rolly as well.

Soon she had scratches on her arms and legs and her T-shirt was soaked with sweat, but even that couldn't distract her from the cold ball of fear in her stomach. Partly to fill the silence and partly to fight her fear with anger, she began talking out loud.

"I don't know why I'm even trying to find you," she said. "You're nothing but a bother anyway. If it weren't for you, my photo album wouldn't have been ruined in that flood and my favorite pair of jeans wouldn't have burned up in the dryer. And I'm sick and tired of always having to hunt you down, too. In fact, maybe we should just leave you out here to find your way home. Maybe that would teach you a lesson—oh!"

Poppy had been doing such a good job working herself up that she hadn't been paying much attention to her surroundings. When she suddenly burst through a thicket of low trees, she was surprised to find herself in a small open area.

The ground was covered with soft grass and wildflowers. The woods had already begun to darken with evening shadows, but a few slanting rays of sunlight filtered through the branches, filling the clearing with the last pieces of the golden afternoon.

Nothing seemed to be moving, not a bird or squirrel, spider or beetle. Even the leaves were still. She glanced up into the trees, half expecting to see a goblin grinning down at her, but she saw only interlacing tree branches and a dark green canopy of leaves that looked almost black in the dusk. The slight breeze that had cooled them off earlier in the day had died away. It was as if she had somehow stumbled into a hidden glade, a place that had fallen under some sort of enchantment.

A shiver rippled across her skin. There was no such thing as magic, of course, no such thing as spells. Even so, she held her breath and listened. Surely, she should be able to hear a truck driving down a road or a car horn blaring. . . .

Instead, she heard a whir overhead and looked up to see bats winging through the air, a steady inky stream against the violet sky. Seconds later, they were gone, and all she could hear was the sound of her own heart pounding.

Suddenly, she realized that she couldn't hear Franny or Will, either. Just minutes ago, they had been close enough that she could hear Franny squeal in dismay when a cobweb brushed across her face.

And now . . . nothing.

The back of her neck prickled. Poppy stood very still. She was absolutely certain that someone—or something—was behind her, watching her.

I should just turn around, she thought. I should be brave, I should turn around and yell, I should scare whoever it is away. Yes, that's exactly what I'll do! On the count of three. One, two, three . . .

She hesitated. What if something really terrible was standing behind her, just waiting for her to turn around before it leaped at her from the shadows?

Don't be ridiculous, she scolded herself. You're letting your imagination run away with you. But if you're that scared, then just run home.

And what about Rolly? Are you really going to leave him with whatever it is you think is lurking in these woods?

Poppy bit her lip. She wanted nothing more than to run home, now, as fast as she could. At the same time, she couldn't help feeling that abandoning Rolly in a dark, scary, bat-filled forest was not the kind of thing big sisters were supposed to do. Not good big sisters, anyway . . .

There was an enormous crash, and Will and Franny came bursting into the clearing, their faces red and sweaty. Franny's ponytail had come loose, and she had twigs and leaves caught in her hair;

Will's T-shirt was ripped, and his sneakers looked as if he'd walked ankle-deep through mud.

"Oh, thank goodness!" Franny said breathlessly. "I was beginning to think you *and* Rolly were lost."

"Why didn't you give a shout?" Will asked irritably. "That was the plan. We all agreed that whoever found him would yell—"

"Oh, who cares?" Franny snapped. "Come on, let's go home."

"What are you guys talking about?" Poppy stared at her brother and sister. "We can't go home without Rolly!"

Now it was Franny and Will's turn to stare at her.

"What are *you* talking about?" Will asked, pointing behind her. "He's right there."

Poppy whirled around. Someone was standing at the edge of the clearing, half hidden in the shadow of a massive oak tree.

"Hello." Rolly stepped forward into the clearing.

A wave of relief washed over Poppy, followed

almost immediately by a wave of anger.

"Rolly, where have you *been*?" she snapped. "We've been looking all over for you."

"I was right here."

"You weren't here a minute ago," she said suspiciously.

"Yes, I was." He smiled sunnily at her. "You just didn't see me."

"Didn't you hear me calling for you?" she said. "Why didn't you let me know where you were?"

"Come on, Poppy," said Franny impatiently. "You found him and he's fine."

"I am so sorry, Poppy," Rolly said, tucking his hand in hers. His eyes shone with tears. "I truly did not mean to scare you. I promise I will never do it again."

Poppy had to resist the urge to pull her hand away. Rolly hadn't cried since he left the crib, and he had refused to hold anyone's hand from the time he could walk.

She looked at Franny and Will, with their messy hair, muddy shoes, and dirty clothes. She glanced down at herself. Her knees were skinned up from crawling through undergrowth, her T-shirt was stained with sweat, and her fingernails were rimmed with dirt. She didn't have to look in a mirror to know that her hair was a mess of tangles.

But Rolly's white shirt was still spotless; his sneakers looked as if they'd just been washed; and his face was clean and bright.

A small, familiar feeling of panic fluttered under her ribs.

Still holding her hand, Rolly started down the trail, so insistently that she was forced to follow.

"Rolly?" she asked. "Are you sure you're all right?"

He stopped and looked up at her. "I'm fine, Poppy," he said. "Let's go home."

Chapter TEN

It took Poppy almost an entire day to figure out that something was very wrong.

It began at breakfast, when Rolly sat at the table without a murmur, ate all his oatmeal without protest, and finished the meal without knocking over his milk glass, spilling his juice, or upending the sugar bowl.

When Franny entered the kitchen, yawning, she saw Rolly and stopped dead in her tracks. "Did you take my hair gel without asking?"

"Franny, please," said Mrs. Malone. "You know how I feel about baseless accusations before breakfast."

"But look at his hair," said Franny. "You can see the comb tracks."

"I think it looks very nice," Mrs. Malone replied.

"Thank you," said Rolly. He patted his head proudly, took a sip of milk, and delicately wiped his mouth with his napkin.

"Well, I'm going to check the bathroom," Franny insisted. "And if I find my hair gel is missing, you are going to get it!" She stalked out of the kitchen.

Rolly gave her a sunny smile as she left and said, "You look nice today, too, Franny."

Will glanced up from the comics section, frowning at Rolly. "What's wrong with you this morning?"

"Nothing at all. I feel quite well," Rolly said cheerfully. "Thank you for asking, Will. May I please be excused from the table?"

Poppy's and Will's eyes met. The only time any of the Malone children asked to be excused was when they were visited by their Great-aunt Agnes (a steely-eyed old lady with strongly expressed opinions about the lack of manners among modern youth).

Surely, Poppy thought, *surely* her parents

would suspect that something was wrong.

But her father was busy rummaging through a drawer for fresh batteries, and her mother was peering at another letter from Oliver Asquith.

"Yes, dear, of course you're excused," said Mrs. Malone. "Oh dear, Oliver's on the run again! He's somewhere in the Balkans now. I haven't had a chance to keep up with the news lately—is that a particularly dangerous area these days?"

"You know what they say," Mr. Malone muttered under his breath. "Hope springs eternal."

Later that day, Rolly volunteered to set the dinner table (a talent previously unsuspected by his family). He picked a handful of wildflowers and presented them as a small bouquet to his mother. He accepted the appearance of liver and onions without a murmur, then ate every bite. And not only did he take a bath, but he seemed to delight in it, lolling in the warm, soapy water until Mrs. Malone told him he would turn into a prune if he stayed in any longer.

Once he was in bed, Poppy went upstairs, intending to brush her teeth, put on her pajamas, and spend an hour or two making notes in her logbook and reading before going to sleep.

But when she got to the bathroom, she froze.

Rolly's bath towel was neatly hung on the rack, rather than lying in a sodden puddle on the floor. As far as she knew, this was an unprecedented event.

She brushed her teeth thoughtfully, then went to her room, where she tried to settle down with the new issue of *Science News Journal*. No matter how hard she tried to focus, however, her attention kept drifting. Something was nagging at her, an uneasy sensation that something had gone very wrong, but she couldn't put her finger on exactly what. . . .

Poppy yawned. Despite her worry, she was getting sleepy. Her eyelids drooped; she felt herself sinking into her nice, comfortable bed; she pulled her fluffy pillow closer and felt herself begin to drift off. . . .

And then, as these things sometimes happen, the answer popped into her head, jolting her awake.

She scrambled out of bed, her heart thumping, turned on her bedside lamp, and pulled *The Little People: A Comprehensive History of Hobgoblins, Pixies, Brownies, and Sprites* from under her mattress. Trembling, she flipped through the book until she found the chapter on goblins. She turned the pages, dense with type, until she found the paragraph that she had only glanced at before.

"Goblins," she read, "have been known to steal a human child and replace it with one of their own children, which are known as gremlins. It is considered a great honor for a gremlin to be chosen as the human child's stand-in. A gremlin sent to live with mortals is what is known as a changeling. Goblins appear to have some talent at shape-shifting, for a gremlin is said to take on the appearance of the human child so convincingly that his or her own parents don't immediately realize that a substitution has been made.

"However, even the most skillful changelings

have been known to slip up in small ways. Parents and family members often become suspicious after a time when they notice small differences in personality and behavior. It's been suggested that one can spot a changeling by looking for the following clues: a changeling may appear wiser and more knowledgeable than a human child of the same age, may have ears that come to a slight but noticeable point, and may demonstrate impeccable manners (having been groomed from an early age in human ways)—"

The book slipped out of Poppy's hands and thudded to the floor. She didn't notice. She stared at the ceiling, trying to convince herself that what she suddenly suspected couldn't possibly be true.

But as much as she tried to argue with herself, one paragraph continued to haunt her:

"Through the centuries, stories have been told about children who seemed to have transformed overnight into someone who was odd or different," the author had written. "Whispers and rumors followed these children around; as they grew up, they were viewed with suspicion by those who feared they were strange beings, wild and mysterious, who perhaps harbored dark plans in what passes for their hearts. These imposters, if indeed they were something other than human, lived out their lives in an atmosphere of loneliness and suspicion. . . ."

The numbers on Poppy's digital clock clicked over. Midnight. The witching hour, when all those things that go bump in the night decide to come out and play . . .

And that was another thing! They hadn't been disturbed by knocking in the walls or crashes in the kitchen for the last two nights. Her parents were so upset that her mother had even dug up the family Ouija board (after swearing everyone to secrecy, since no self-respecting parapsychologist would use a children's toy for research) and organized an impromptu attempt to contact the Dark Presence.

"Close your eyes," Mrs. Malone had commanded. "I'm dimming the lights. Now, everyone place your fingers on the planchette and concentrate! Perhaps we can entice the Dark Presence to appear by sending out mental vibrations of welcome—"

"Why should we ask some stupid ghost who dumps flour on people's heads to come back?" muttered Franny, who knew how to carry a grudge.

"I like sleeping through the night," Will had murmured. "The longer the Dark Presence stays away, the better."

"Shh!" Mrs. Malone had said. "Honestly, you both know better than to say things like that! Spirits can be quite sensitive to negative vibrations, so let's all take a deep, cleansing breath and think positive thoughts. . . ."

But the Dark Presence had remained stubbornly silent, not just on that evening, but for the last three days.

Almost since the day they moved in, the nights had been filled with strange noises and the days had been filled with petty annoyances.

Now, suddenly, life was back to normal. Why?

Poppy flopped over and punched her pillow a few times.

Why would the goblins suddenly give up and go home?

She tried to come up with sensible, reassuring reasons—they were tired of playing pranks, they had moved on to another house, they had suddenly reformed and vowed to do only good in the world, there was no such thing as goblins—but none of them were remotely convincing.

There seemed to be only one logical reason for the goblins to have disappeared: because they had gotten what they wanted.

Chapter
ELEVEN

Poppy thought she was far too worried to fall asleep, but she must have been wrong because she was startled awake some time after midnight by a frenzied pounding on the front door.

She got out of bed and went into the hall just as Mrs. Malone appeared, blinking and pulling on her robe. Although she had clearly been awakened from a deep sleep, her voice was bright with hope as she glanced back into her bedroom. "Emerson, did you hear that? I think the séance worked! The Dark Presence has returned!"

Poppy heard a mighty snort from her parents' bedroom, which meant that her father had just awoken from a sound sleep. "Wha—?"

Mrs. Malone raised her voice. "The Dark Presence, I said! It's back!"

"Wha—?" There was a crash of glass (which Poppy successfully interpreted as the sound of her father searching for his glasses with a wildly waving hand and knocking over a bedside lamp), then Mr. Malone called out, "Wait . . . ouch! Wait for me . . . don't face the spirits alone, Lucille!"

But Mrs. Malone sped down the hall past Poppy, knocking a rapid tattoo on Will's and Franny's doors as she went and caroling, "Get up, get up, it's time to go to work! Our ghost has returned!"

She was on the landing before Franny staggered out of her room, her head covered with curlers. And she was halfway down the stairs by the time Will's door opened and he emerged, weaving slightly, his eyes half closed. "I was having a dream," he murmured sadly. "And it was a really good dream, too. . . ."

He was interrupted by another pounding at the front door, more frantic this time.

"Don't answer it, Lucille!" Mr. Malone called

out. "You know how moody ghosts can be—"

"Nonsense, Emerson, this is the first contact we've had in days!" Mrs. Malone called back over her shoulder before speeding down the last few steps and flinging open the door.

There was no ghost standing on the porch. Instead, there was a man who was very much alive and seemed to be in great distress. His dark wavy hair was disarranged (although in a dashing kind of way), his eyes were shadowed with fatigue (which only made his blue eyes look brighter), and his shirt and khaki pants were dirty and torn (in a picturesque way that seemed to hint at death-defying adventures).

"Lucille!" he cried, his face lighting up. "Thank goodness you're home!"

"Oliver Asquith!" said Mrs. Malone. "What on earth are you doing here? And what happened to you?"

Oliver Asquith closed his eyes and put one hand on the doorframe, as if to support himself. "What happened to me?" he echoed in a hollow voice.

"Horrible things. Vile things. *Unspeakable* things."

Somehow, in spite of the fact that he seemed almost too weak to stand, he managed to pitch his voice so that it could be heard quite clearly, even on the second-floor landing. Poppy suddenly felt that she was in the balcony of a theater, looking down at a stage. For the moment, she forgot her worry about Rolly and watched with interest as Oliver Asquith clutched the doorframe, sighed a deep, shuddery sigh, then opened his eyes to look beseechingly at Mrs. Malone. "May I come in?"

"Of course, Oliver," said Mrs. Malone. "You don't need to ask!"

He picked up a stained duffle bag and staggered inside. Once the door was safely closed behind him, he delicately pulled the curtain aside and peered out at the street. "I think I've managed to outrun them," he said. "At least for now."

Oliver Asquith turned back to Mrs. Malone and took one of her hands between both of his. "I'm so very sorry to intrude," he murmured. "But I didn't know where else to turn."

"I don't suppose a hotel ever crossed your mind," muttered Mr. Malone just as Franny drifted sleepily to the landing to join them.

"What's going on?" she said, looking over Poppy's shoulder.

"Shh." Will was watching the scene below, his eyes bright with interest. "Professor Asquith just showed up, and he looks like he's in trouble."

Franny let out a squeak of dismay. "Why didn't you tell me who it was?" she whispered. "I need to change my clothes . . . put on some mascara . . . oh, and my *hair* . . ." She ran back to her room, clutching her head.

Mr. Malone descended the staircase in a grand manner, stopping on the last step so that he could look down on their midnight visitor.

"Oliver," he said coolly. "How nice to see you again. I thought we'd lost you somewhere in Carpathia."

Oliver Asquith ran one hand through his thick, wavy hair. Somehow, he managed to convey, in that one weary gesture, that he had suffered greatly but was bravely carrying on.

"Emerson," he said in a rich, fruity voice. "How good of you to offer me sanctuary."

"Sanctuary might be going a bit far," said Mr. Malone. "Let's start with a bed and see how things go from there. What exactly is the problem?"

Oliver shrugged. "Just a little trouble I ran into in Moldavia," he said. "I think I mentioned it in one of my letters?"

"Yes, I believe you did," said Mr. Malone. "It was a bit more than a little trouble, though, wasn't it? Your research assistant was found dead and decapitated."

"Oh yes. Right," said Oliver. He looked slightly taken aback, as if he'd momentarily forgotten what had happened to his research assistant or, indeed, that he'd ever had one. He quickly recovered himself and said, "Yes, yes, that was indeed tragic. But what I'm referring to is what happened afterward. You see, I'd been making great inroads with one particular member of the vampire cult. He was willing to tell me everything. He had even agreed to be filmed for the series. But then a few of his comrades found out that he planned to Tell All and, well . . ."

"Now you've arrived on our doorstep with Moldavian vampires on your tail," Mr. Malone finished.

"Perhaps we could try to look at the bright side?" Mrs. Malone suggested. "Perhaps we could focus our energies on the positive?"

"I fail to see anything positive about having dozens of blood-sucking members of the undead descending upon us," said Mr. Malone. "Especially when there are children in the home—"

"Oh, Emerson, *please*," said Mrs. Malone. "We've let the children take part in voodoo ceremonies, go scuba diving in Loch Ness, and track the Moth Man through New Jersey swamps! I hardly think a few vampires could be any more dangerous than that."

But Oliver Asquith held up a hand and said in a hollow voice, "No, no, Emerson has a point. It's one thing for me to risk my own life in the pursuit of scientific advancement. But the two of you have so much to lose these days—" He looked around at the grandfather clock in the hall, the rug on the floor, the framed pictures on the walls, and smiled faintly. "You've really settled down, haven't you, Emerson? I completely understand if you've lost your taste for danger—"

Mr. Malone bristled. "Let me remind you that I once confronted El Chupacabra in a remote Mexican jungle, armed only with a walking stick and the can of foot powder that I happened to have in my luggage. I'm simply thinking about the children—"

"Of course." Oliver Asquith let out a deep sigh, then bowed his head in resignation. "You're quite right. I should go."

Mrs. Malone clutched her robe even more tightly around her. "Nonsense!" she cried. "If something happened to you, Emerson and I would never forgive ourselves! Would we, Emerson?"

There was a short, awkward silence. Finally, Mr. Malone said, "Well, 'never' is a bit strong, but it would certainly take a few months—" He caught his wife's eye and finished hastily, "Lucille is right. You must stay."

Oliver Asquith drooped with relief. "You're too kind. I don't know how I'll ever repay you, but I promise you"—he grasped Mrs. Malone's hands, held them over his heart, and peered soulfully into her eyes—"I promise you that I shall!"

Mrs. Malone blushed and let out a small laugh that was almost a titter.

Will made a gagging sound behind Poppy's left shoulder. She stepped back on his toe, hard, but it was too late.

Her mother looked up, saw them on the landing, and frowned. "What are you children doing up? It's almost one o'clock in the morning. You should be asleep."

"But I want to hear about the vampires," Franny said breathlessly. She was hanging over the banister, her newly brushed hair gleaming in the low light. She flashed a bright smile that showed off her dimples to their best advantage. "Hello, Professor

Asquith! It sounds as if you've been having the most *amazing* adventures. We'd all simply *love* to hear about them. . . ."

Mr. Malone made a growling noise. "Not tonight," he said. "Go back to bed. All of you."

"But I'm not tired at all," Franny protested, tossing her hair. "Mom, can't we please stay up and hear about the vampires?"

Mrs. Malone hesitated. "Maybe tomorrow," she said. Her children groaned, and she said more firmly, "Oliver will still be here in the morning. Now off to bed, all of you!"

As Poppy, Will, and Franny trailed down the hall, she turned to Oliver and said, "Come into the kitchen. I'll make some sandwiches and coffee, and you can tell us all about what's been happening to you since your last letter. . . ."

"We can stay up until dawn when they want us to run infrared cameras," Franny muttered, "but all of a sudden we're growing children who need our sleep. It's not fair."

"Totally inconsistent parenting," Will agreed.

"We'll all need years of therapy to get over it." He yawned hugely, then drifted down the hall toward his bedroom. "G'night."

Poppy paused by Rolly's bedroom. On a sudden impulse, she opened the door.

Moonlight slanted into the room through a gap in the curtains, turning the familiar space, with its twin bed, dresser, and toy box, a mysterious blue. Rolly was fast asleep. This should have been a reassuring sight, but it was not. He was lying on his back, as straight as an arrow, his arms at his sides. The sheet and quilt were pulled neatly up under his chin, and he had a sweet smile on his face.

"Will," Poppy called softly. "Come here for a second."

Will reluctantly drifted back to Rolly's room. "What's up?" he asked, blinking. "You look like you've seen a ghost."

Before she could answer, he added, "And if you did, please keep quiet about it. We've already got the Dark Presence to deal with. Now we're probably going to be attacked by Moldavian vampires."

"Take a look at Rolly," Poppy said, easing the door open a little wider. "Do you notice anything strange about him?"

Will glanced at the bed. "No. Do you?"

"Well, yes. He looks so calm. So quiet. So, so . . . *sweet*. It's unnatural."

"It's a statistical aberration." Will shrugged. "Enjoy it while it lasts."

"Okay, but—" Poppy began, but Will was already headed down the hall.

"At least he's not experimenting with lighter fluid," he called back over his shoulder before disappearing into his room.

Poppy was alone. After a moment, she gave herself a little shake, then she strode across the room to Rolly's bed. She gently brushed back his hair, revealing his left ear. It was as perfect and pink and curved as a seashell, the most normal ear one could imagine. There wasn't anything pointy about it at all.

Poppy let out a sigh of relief.

Honestly, you should know better than to let

some silly book get you in a state, she told herself. If you don't watch it, you'll end up on someone's doorstep in twenty years, wild-eyed and claiming that vampires are chasing you.

Still, she took one last look at Rolly before she shut the door.

He was smiling in his sleep, a smile so angelic that he looked as if he belonged on a Christmas card.

It should have been a heartwarming sight, but Poppy shivered all the same.

Chapter
TWELVE

Poppy woke up the next morning in the middle of a confused dream involving a vampire who was chasing a goblin who looked an awful lot like Rolly. She jumped out of bed, determined to tell her parents about her suspicions. Who cared if they called a television station or the local newspaper? One good thing about her parents, unlike many others—they were sure to believe her when she told them their youngest child had been stolen by goblins.

But when she burst into the kitchen, she found that the rest of the family was already there, engrossed in listening to Oliver Asquith. At least, her mother and Franny were apparently enraptured. Mrs. Malone's eyes were shining with admiration; Franny's chin was propped on one hand, and her gaze was fixed unblinkingly on Oliver's face. (Poppy noticed that Franny had apparently decided to wear the contents of her jewelry box in honor of the occasion; she had a sparkly gold barrette in her hair, her favorite necklace, tinselly earrings from last Christmas, and three rings on each hand.) Even Will and Rolly were caught up in what their visitor was saying. Will's fork had paused halfway to his mouth, and Rolly was listening politely as he neatly cut a sausage into small bites.

Only Mr. Malone was resisting the lure of high drama, artfully told. He had retreated behind the front section of the newspaper and was pretending to read. Only the occasional rustle of paper, caused by his fists clenching, betrayed his true emotions.

"And that was when I realized that I had to flee for my life," Oliver was saying as Poppy took her place at the table.

"What an amazing story," Mrs. Malone said breathlessly. "How lucky that you still had that vial of holy water in your coat pocket!"

Most people who had survived a near-death experience and were now dealing with a flock of vampires bent on revenge would have little appetite for breakfast, Poppy thought, but Oliver Asquith was clearly made of stronger stuff. A plate with a few remnants of scrambled eggs and hash browns sat in front of him, and toast crumbs were scattered on the tablecloth. He lifted his cup to his lips, then glanced down as if astonished to find that it was empty.

"I wonder . . ." He gazed vaguely around the kitchen. "I wonder if perhaps there's any coffee left?"

"I'll get you some," said Franny, leaping to her feet. She grabbed the coffeepot and began pouring him another cup.

"Thank you, that's very kind," said Professor Asquith, bestowing such a glittering smile on her that she blushed and forgot to stop pouring.

After a brief interlude for flustered apologies and mopping-up operations, Oliver continued his story.

"Anyway, as I was saying . . . I fled, hoping against hope that the vampires would not be able to pick up my trail. I followed all the proper protocols, of course—scattered salt on my footprints, drew crosses on every door I walked through—but they have been far more resourceful than I had anticipated. Now that you've taken me in, I'm afraid we must prepare ourselves to fend off a full-scale invasion of the undead."

He sat back in his chair with the self-satisfied air of someone who has successfully foisted a problem off on someone else. "Does anyone else want more toast?"

Professor Asquith generously offered to make the toast. He was relying too much on their hospitality as it was, he said. He couldn't let Franny and Mrs. Malone do all the work, he declared. He would take his turn at the toaster, he insisted.

Then he tried to stand up, gasped, and sank back into his chair.

"Oliver, what is it?" asked Mrs. Malone.

"Oh, nothing, really." He bit his lip, clearly trying to mask the pain. "It's just a . . . well, I suppose you might call it an old war wound, in a way. I got it when I was on the trail of the Vrykolakas; it has a tendency to flare up at the most inconvenient times."

There was a snort from behind the newspaper. Mr. Malone muttered something about injuries that suddenly appeared when there was work to be done, but fortunately his mutter was so indistinct they could all pretend to ignore it.

"Don't worry, I can make the toast," said Franny, springing into action. "What are the Vrykolakas?"

"Greek vampires," Oliver Asquith explained. "They've been hanging around since the time of Homer. Completely vicious, of course, but rather charming in their own way. Interestingly enough, they're the only type of vampire that actually likes garlic." He took a sip of coffee and added thoughtfully, "I remember a certain young lady who had a gift for making moussaka that bordered on genius; I still regret what the world lost when I was forced to drive a stake through her heart."

Poppy was too well-mannered to roll her eyes at a guest, but she caught Will's eye and raised one eyebrow a fraction of an inch. The corner of his mouth turned up, then he put on his most earnest expression and said, "So how did you get hurt, Professor Asquith?"

Oliver shrugged modestly. "Oh, the usual thing. I had to make an unexpectedly fast exit from a crypt at the base of Mount Penteli. I was planning to open a certain coffin before the sun set but, as luck would have it, my watch battery was running down and I ended up staying just a few minutes too long. I didn't know anything was wrong until the coffin lid opened and I was face-to-face with a particularly large and gruesome Vrykolakas specimen. The next thing I knew—"

"Franny!" Poppy yelled. "The toast!"

"Oh! Oh dear!" Franny stared at the smoking toaster in dismay. "I'm so sorry, I'll make some more, can someone hand me the bread . . . ?"

But before anyone could do so, the smoke alarm went off with an ear-piercing shriek. Franny began flapping a dish towel in the air. Will informed her that was absolutely the wrong way to get rid of smoke and suggested that she open the door instead. Franny suggested that, if he was so smart, perhaps *he* should open the door. Mrs. Malone tried to take the toast out of the toaster, burned her fingers, and dropped it to the floor, where it shattered into crumbs.

"Dear me, what drama," Mr. Malone said from behind his newspaper. "No wonder your TV viewers are enthralled."

Oliver Asquith did not rise to this bait, however. He simply waited calmly until the alarm had been deactivated, the floor had been swept, more toast had been made, and his audience was seated around the kitchen table once more before continuing. "As I was saying, I was racing out the crypt's entrance, just steps ahead of the vampire, when I slipped and fell, badly twisting my ankle." He shook his head. "It still gives me trouble on damp days, but one must soldier on, of course."

Franny and Mrs. Malone sighed in unison, causing Mr. Malone to turn to the sports page with an irritable rustle. "Too bad there weren't any reporters there to capture the moment," he said. "I can see the headline now: 'World-Famous Paranormal Investigator Trips on Step; Develops Slight Limp.'"

"I wouldn't mind meeting a vampire," said Franny. "Especially if he was young and handsome and terribly, terribly tormented about being undead—"

Mr. Malone snorted. "For your future reference, any handsome young vampire you may meet is only thinking about one thing—"

"Emerson," said Mrs. Malone.

"How to drain you of every drop of blood in your body," he finished. "For the last time, Franny: vampires are cold, heartless, evil creatures. They are not *dreamy*!"

"And they don't exist," Poppy added. "Minor point."

"Ah yes, you're the budding skeptic, aren't you, Poppy?" Oliver Asquith gave a knowing chuckle that made Poppy yearn to throw the butter at his head. "We all go through that phase at some point in our youth, don't we, Emerson? You'll soon learn that there are more things in heaven and earth than you can dream of—"

"Yes," said Mr. Malone. "For example, I find it quite odd that these alleged vampires were able to follow you across the Atlantic. After all, it's a well-known fact that vampires can't travel over water."

"You don't still believe that old wives' tale, do you, Emerson?" Oliver Asquith asked in amazement. He smiled blandly at Mr. Malone as he buttered another piece of toast. "I suppose family life has prevented you from keeping up on the latest research."

Mr. Malone lowered his newspaper, the better to glare at his guest. "I have investigated the Obayifo in Ghana, the Yara-Ma-Yha-Who in

Australia, and the Chiang-Shi in the Gansu province of China," he said stiffly. "I don't need to read every obscure little journal to know all I need to know about vampires."

Oliver Asquith shrugged. "Well, you'll soon have a chance to put your theories to the test," he said briskly. "I predict we'll see the first *drakolai* by tomorrow at sundown. That only gives us about thirty-two hours to get ready for them, so we'd better build up our strength while we can." He rubbed his hands and looked over the breakfast table. "I don't suppose there's more bacon?"

"I'm not sure how much we have left. . . ." said Mrs. Malone.

Will grinned. "But if we need more, I'm sure Franny would be willing to go out and butcher a pig," he said. "Really, it wouldn't be any trouble at all. . . ."

"There are still a few slices in the package," said Franny, giving her brother a warning look. She turned to Oliver and smiled. "How many pieces would you like?"

"Two would just about hit the spot," said Oliver Asquith. "Well, as long as you're up . . . perhaps three?"

"You don't expect us to believe that goblins are real," said Franny later that afternoon. "For heaven's sake, Poppy. You're supposed to be the scientist in the family."

"I wouldn't have told you about the goblins if I didn't have proof," said Poppy.

"Even if goblins do exist, why would they want Rolly?" Will asked reasonably. "Why would *anyone* want Rolly?"

"I don't know," Poppy snapped. "I just know that they took him."

She fanned herself irritably with the 1972 issue of *Popular Mechanics* that she'd found hidden behind the upturned bucket she was sitting on. They had decided to hold their council of war in the toolshed, safely out of their parents' sight. They were afraid of being recruited to either fortify the house against vampires, hunt for the still-lurking

Dark Presence, or track ley lines in the hot sun. The shed door stood half open to let a little air inside, but the atmosphere was still sweltering.

Poppy looked from Will, who was stretched out on the floor and appeared ready to fall asleep despite the fact the floor was concrete, to Franny, who was draped over an ancient armchair that was rubbed bald in places and losing its stuffing. They wore identical expressions that managed to combine complete skepticism and increasing worry.

She took a deep breath and decided to try making her case again, building it slowly with logic and evidence and reason. "Look, I know this is hard to believe. But please, try to keep an open mind—"

"You sound like Dad." Will yawned.

"I do not!" Poppy kicked his ankle, a little harder than she meant to.

"Ow." He opened one eye, squinted disapprovingly at her, then closed it again. "*Exactly* like Dad," he murmured sleepily to himself.

"Don't be ridiculous—"

"Will's right," said Franny. "Every time we're on a case and Dad's gotten to the part of the investigation where he's ready to reveal his Theory of What's Really Going On If Only We Could See the Truth, that's what he says. 'Please try to keep an open mind.'" She rolled her eyes. "And then if you try to tell him what's wrong with his theory, he always says, 'Don't be ridiculous.'"

Franny pulled the elastic band out of her hair and redid her ponytail, her head tilted at the perfect angle in order to look through the doorway to where Oliver Asquith was sitting at his ease in a lawn chair, a tall glass of iced tea in one hand and a paperback mystery in the other.

"He's so handsome, isn't he?" Franny sighed. "And smart and adventurous and brave—"

"And a good eater," Will added. "Don't forget to add that to the list."

"I don't know why you have to be so sarcastic all the time," said Franny. "After all he's been through, he needs to get his strength back—"

"He must have the strength of three people by

now," Will pointed out. "Considering how much he ate at breakfast."

Poppy waved her hand to get their attention. "Excuse me? We're drifting," she said. "We were talking about Rolly."

"Oh, right." Reluctantly, Will opened his eyes and sat up. "So you're saying that a goblin took Rolly and then another goblin who looks exactly like him took his place. A—what did you call it?"

"A changeling. A goblin who replaces a human child and is raised by the unwitting human parents—"

"Lucille, come quick!" Mr. Malone's shout interrupted her. "I just felt an incredibly strong energy surge! I may have located the central vortex!"

Mr. Malone zigzagged into view, his outstretched dowsing rod quivering in his hands. He looked as if he were being pulled across the lawn by an enormous invisible dog.

"Unwitting is right," said Will. "I bet it turns out we're adopted."

"I'm sorry, dear, I'm in the middle of something

important," Mrs. Malone called back from an open second-story window. She held up a small cloth bundle. "I've got the garlic all ready, Oliver!"

Professor Asquith looked up from his novel and raised his glass in salute. "Intrepid woman!" he said. "I wish I'd had you at my side during that nasty business in Slovakia!"

"Too bad it wasn't nastier," Mr. Malone muttered, casting a dark look at their guest. "Too bad you aren't still in Slovakia. . . ." All the energy seemed to have drained out of his ley line. He wandered listlessly toward the corner of the house and then out of sight.

"I made twenty-three bundles with three cloves each," Mrs. Malone called out. "That's enough to hang over every window and door in the house—"

"Don't forget the chimney," Oliver reminded her as he languidly turned a page of his novel. "Vampires will use any opening to get inside, you know. They *count* on people forgetting about the chimneys."

"Oh yes, of course." Mrs. Malone was hanging halfway out the window as she tried to nail the garlic bundle to the frame over her head. "Let me know when it's centered."

"A little more to the left, I think," Oliver called back. "No, no, that's too far. Try an inch or so to the right. . . ."

"I can't believe we're going to have to live in a house that reeks of garlic," said Franny. "I'm going to have to take three showers a day just to make sure I don't smell like a pizza."

At that moment, Rolly came out the back door, carrying a soccer ball. His shirt and shorts looked as clean and fresh as when he'd put them on in the morning. His hair was neatly combed and his face was scrubbed pink.

"See what I mean?" Poppy asked. "That doesn't look at all like Rolly."

She could feel her sister and brother exchange a look behind her back.

"Actually," said Franny carefully, "he looks exactly like Rolly."

"Only cleaner," Will added. "And less diabolical."

"That's my point!" Poppy said between gritted teeth. "That's what I've been *saying*. Last night he put his dirty clothes in the hamper, picked up his toys, spent an hour drawing pictures with colored markers and never once wrote on the wall—"

Franny tilted her head to one side, considering this. "He *has* been really good lately."

"Lately, as in *for the last twenty-four hours*," Poppy said, pressing her point. "*After* he got lost in the woods." She could tell from Will's and Franny's faces that they were almost convinced. She sat up a little straighter and said, "That's when I think the exchange was made."

Franny raised an eyebrow. Will pressed his lips together. Poppy knew that she'd lost them.

"Maybe he's finally growing up," Franny suggested. "Stranger things have happened."

"I saw the goblin," Poppy said. "I talked to it. I took photos—"

"Yeah, and what happened to them?" Will

asked. "Let me guess. The goblins destroyed them."

"They did!"

Will shook his head. "Come on. No one will buy that story."

Poppy slumped down, her elbows on her knees. "Forget it," she said.

"Listen, Poppy," said Franny. "If you're so sure that Rolly has been stolen by goblins, why haven't you told Mom and Dad?"

Just at that moment, Mr. Malone came back around the house and began circling Oliver Asquith's lawn chair with his dowsing rod.

"I hope your ankle is feeling better," he said.

"Much better, thank you," said Oliver Asquith.

"Perhaps you'd like to try your hand with one of the dowsing rods you sent us? We've really just scratched the surface—"

"I wish I could," said Oliver Asquith, "but I fear I might throw out my back. I felt a definite twinge this morning when I got up, and I know from experience that one can't be too careful—"

"How does this look?" Mrs. Malone had finally

181

managed to nail a garlic bundle to the center of the windowframe. She beamed down at Professor Asquith, her face scarlet and her hair straggling across her cheeks in damp strands. "All we have to do is finish off the rest of the windows, scatter some salt on the porch, and nail iron horseshoes on the doors, and we'll be ready for anything!" She spotted Mr. Malone for the first time. "Oh, there you are, Emerson. I wondered where you had disappeared to."

Mr. Malone stiffened. "You might just possibly be interested in knowing that I think I've detected a slight but definite energy flux warp by the oleander bushes." Even from a distance, it was clear he was gritting his teeth. "I know fluctuations in the space-time continuum aren't *quite* as newsworthy as vampires, but perhaps I can get a small mention in an academic journal somewhere. . . ."

Poppy turned back to her sister and brother. "Do you think I should talk to them before the vampire attack or wait until after Dad finds the energy vortex?"

Franny and Will looked at their parents, then at each other, then at Poppy.

"Okay," said Will. "I still think you're nuts, but if it will make you feel better to go goblin hunting, I'm in."

Poppy nodded her thanks, then looked at Franny.

"Well, I'm certainly not going to let the two of you go off and leave me behind to hang garlic with Mom," she said. "I'm not an idiot, for heaven's sake."

That evening, as the supper dishes were being cleared from the table, Mrs. Malone announced that Rolly had to go to bed early.

"We don't know what tonight will bring," she said. "I want you to be tucked in, safe and sound. Now don't argue with me, Rolly. I simply can't be worrying about you *and* Moldavian vampires—"

"I'll be glad to go to bed early, Mother." He gave her a sunny smile. "I understand that you have to concentrate on your work. And I am"—he yawned hugely—"I *am* rather tired."

"Oh." Mrs. Malone seemed both pleased and somewhat taken aback by this. "Well, good. Let's get your bath ready, then." She gazed vaguely around the room. "Now, whose turn is it to do the dishes?"

Mr. Malone stood up, his chair scraping across the floor, and headed for the door. "I think I'd better check the outside of the house one more time before night falls," he said hastily. "Just to make sure there aren't any unprotected spots where a vampire could slip through. . . ."

"I do know a *bit* about setting up perimeter defenses, Emerson," Oliver Asquith said, following Mr. Emerson out the door. "It was the only thing that saved me from Cihuateteo three years ago, when I went to Mexico to research Aztec legends of the undead—"

As the door closed behind them, Franny slipped out the room, murmuring something about how it couldn't possibly be her turn to clear the table since she had been forced to do the breakfast dishes that very morning, and Poppy and Will were left alone.

"See what I mean?" Poppy asked. "When did Rolly ever talk like that?"

Will shrugged, staring glumly at the table of dirty dishes. "He is acting weird," he admitted. "But Rolly always acts weird. Maybe this is just a different kind of weird."

"Come on," said Poppy, deciding not to argue. "Let's hurry up and do the dishes so we can get ready. I've still got to pack my backpack and we're going to have to find the perfect moment to sneak away. . . ."

But Will stayed seated as she stacked up several plates and carried them to the sink.

"How interesting," he whispered, pressing his fingers to his forehead and closing his eyes. "I seem to be getting another vision—hey!"

His eyes popped open in time to see Poppy at the sink. She was pointing the rinsing sprayer at his face and grinning.

"Don't even try it," she warned.

* * *

Poppy slipped down the hall and quietly opened the door to Rolly's room. Although it was still light outside, the curtains had been drawn, and it took a moment for her eyes to adjust to the dimness. When they did, she saw that the bedcovers had been turned back, but Rolly wasn't asleep or in bed. Instead, he was curled up on the windowseat with a book in his lap.

Even from the doorway, she recognized it. He was reading her book on the little people. He must have snuck into her room to take it.

She was ready to stride across the room and snatch it from his hands. In fact, she had even taken two furious steps when a tiny sound stopped her in her tracks.

It was the sound of a sniffle.

Poppy tiptoed closer. "Are you all right?" she whispered.

He hastily wiped his face with his sleeve. "I'm fine."

She sat down on his bed. "Look," she began. "I

know you're not Rolly. So who are you, really?"

"I'm not *really*," he said, giggling. "I'm *Rolly*."

Poppy felt a chill run down her spine. Rolly had come into the world scowling and had set about developing a remarkably somber personality. It was completely unlike him to make a joke, even a weak one. And he never, ever giggled.

"You know what I mean!" she pressed on. "Where did you come from?"

He looked puzzled. "What do you mean?"

"Before you were here, in this house," said Poppy. "You were somewhere else, right? That other place, the place where you were before you came here, we want to know where that place was."

Rolly's beady black eyes gazed steadily at her. "I have always been here," he said simply.

He looks just like Rolly, she seemed to hear Will and Franny say. *He acts just like Rolly. . . .*

"I've always lived here with you and Franny and Will and Mother and Father—"

Poppy raised her eyebrows. "Mother and Father?"

187

He looked suddenly wary. "Yes. I mean—" He bit his lip. Poppy could practically see him mentally replaying what he had just said and searching his memory for the right words.

Then his face relaxed and, with a note of relief in his voice, he said, "Mom and Dad." He nodded to himself. "I've always lived here with you and Franny and Will and *Mom and Dad*."

"Look." Poppy sat cross-legged on the floor so that she was face-to-face with him. "You're not going to get in trouble. I just want you to tell the truth, that's all."

An amused, almost sly look crossed the changeling's face. For a split second, he looked not like a little boy at all, but like an ancient member of an alien race.

Then his expression shifted again to one of baffled innocence. "I *am* telling you the truth," he insisted.

Poppy hesitated. More than anything else, his stubborn refusal to break under interrogation came close to convincing her that this was actually

Rolly. A memory flashed into her mind of her father giving Rolly a jaundiced look and saying, "I almost look forward to seeing That Boy on the witness stand some day. He'll make mincemeat of the best prosecutor the legal system can throw at him."

Then her gaze fell on the book, which was open to the illustration of a goblin. The goblin wore a long dress and a kerchief over her hair, and was stirring a pot of stew over a fire. She didn't seem motherly, exactly—her eyes were too sharp and her fingernails too long and pointed—but Poppy had seen the changeling's chin tremble when he stared at the picture.

"Is that your mother?" she asked gently.

"No," he said, slamming the book shut.

"You must miss her," persisted Poppy. "You must wish that you could see her again. . . ."

He set his chin. "I don't know what you're talking about."

"Don't you wish you could see her again?"

He blinked, as if trying not to cry.

"Don't you want to go home?"

She saw a shadow of some feeling, something like homesickness, pass over his face. He turned to stare out the dark window.

"Home?" he asked in a wavering voice.

Poppy held her breath. She felt that she was just about to break through. All he needed was a little push. . . .

Then an enormous moth, as pale as a ghost, crashed into the window. The changeling jerked back in surprise, and the spell was broken.

He turned away from the moonlit night and looked calmly into her eyes.

"I *am* home, Poppy," he said. "And I'm never going to leave."

Chapter
THIRTEEN

"**I** don't know why we have to traipse through the woods in this sweltering heat," Franny complained, swatting at a bug that was merrily circling her head and making occasional daring dives toward her nose. "Why can't we wait until it cools off a little?"

"Because that won't happen until October," Poppy snapped. "And waiting four months to start an investigation probably isn't the best way to solve a kidnapping."

"You don't have to be so sarcastic," said Franny. "I was just *asking*."

Poppy bit her tongue. The last thing she wanted to do was start an argument, which was exactly what would happen if she said what was on her mind. There were three things making her cranky. First, she was just as hot, sweaty, and thirsty as Will and Franny; in fact, she was probably even hotter, sweatier, and thirstier because she happened to be the only member of this expedition carrying a backpack. That led to the second reason she was cranky: despite her best efforts, she had not been able to convince Will and Franny to carry their fair share of the emergency supplies she had collected.

"We're going for a walk," Franny had said. "And it's still light out, for heaven's sake. Nothing dangerous is going to happen."

"That's what people always say," Poppy had pointed out. "Right before something dangerous happens. *Then* they wish they had some equipment. *Then* they wish they had thought ahead."

"Look, I can understand carrying a water bottle," Will had said, peering into her backpack. "But you've got three flashlights, a box of matches and a lighter, sweaters, gloves, long-sleeved shirts, six light sticks, a first-aid kit, a nightscope, extra socks, a bandanna, a rope, candles, and—hey!" He pulled an energy bar out of a side pocket. "Chocolate chip!"

She had snatched it back. "These are emergency supplies. Which means that we use them only in the case of an *emergency*. Like when we're lost in a dark woods with nothing else standing between us and a slow death from starvation."

"*So* dramatic," murmured Franny (which was, Poppy thought, a fine example of the pot calling the kettle black).

"We have to be ready for anything," said Poppy. "We have to be prepared."

"Fine," Franny snapped. "So we're ready for anything—so what? Even if goblins do exist, how do you know where to look for them?"

"I have a hunch," Poppy said shortly, scratching her elbow.

"A hunch!" Will said. "You're getting to be as bad as Mom and Dad. Next thing you know, you'll be having some of those strange tingly feelings that mean that something uncanny is approaching.

Whatever happened to evidence? Whatever happened to logic and reason and the principles of scientific inquiry? Whatever happened to—"

"You can go home if you want," Poppy snapped. She plowed through a particularly prickly section of bushes, then wished she hadn't. "Ow."

She stopped and pushed damp hair off her forehead. They had almost reached the clearing where they had found Rolly. If a switch had taken place, she thought, it must have been there. . . .

"I think we're just wasting our time," said Franny. "All because you have a hunch."

"Would you rather be back at the house, hanging cloves of garlic?" Poppy asked impatiently. "Or setting up more infrared cameras to take pictures of the Dark Presence?"

"You're right, Poppy," said Will sarcastically. "Mom and Dad are wasting their time looking for vampires and ghosts. We, on the other hand, know what we're doing. We're looking for *goblins*!"

Poppy glared at him. "This is completely different," she said before stalking down the trail.

Even as she walked away, she knew why she was feeling so angry. It was reason number three: she was beginning to think that she might actually be wrong.

They had now spent two hours in the woods. Poppy had counted sixteen new mosquito bites. Franny had flicked off three spiders and now kept brushing anxiously at her hair every ten seconds. Even Will, who normally didn't mind bugs or dirt or getting sweaty, was beginning to look frayed around the edges.

Worse, they had found no trace of goblins. In fact, they hadn't found any clues at all.

Poppy hated to admit it, but she was beginning to suspect that she had missed something major, some incredibly obvious clue, that she had been outsmarted by the goblins. Maybe they were spending all their time looking in the wrong places . . . they could spend days, months, years looking in all the wrong places. After all, there was (by definition) only one right place to look and millions of wrong places.

Behind her, Franny suddenly let out a squeal and began batting at her head. "Oh, ugh, get it off me!"

"What's wrong now?" asked Will. He looked at her hair, finally pulling off a small leaf. He held it up in front of her face. "Oh, I see. You were attacked by a crazed leaf." He tossed it on the ground. "No need to thank me."

Franny glared at him, then at Poppy. "I hate bugs, I hate spiders, I hate nature, I hate being outside, I hate being hot, I hate sweating, and I hate doing something that is completely stupid."

"You know what your problem is, Franny?" asked Will. "You're always holding back. You need to learn to express yourself more."

"Ha-ha," said Franny. "Let's face it, Poppy's got us worked up for nothing. I bet this whole thing is just one of Rolly's tricks."

Poppy didn't bother to respond to this. She knelt down and studied the ground.

"What are you looking for?" Franny asked. "Why did you stop here?"

"I'm searching for clues," Poppy said absently.

"Clues?" Franny scoffed. "What kind of clue could we possibly find in this wilderness? There's nothing here but dirt and bugs and rocks and—"

"And this." Poppy delicately brushed a few leaves to the side of the trail. Gleaming up at them from the dirt was a crumpled piece of gold paper.

"That's a wrapper from a Choc-O-Bomb," said Will, crouching beside her. "It must have fallen from Rolly's pocket."

"So?" Franny stood with her arms folded. She still looked cross. "He could have dropped it the other day."

"Look, there's another one!" Will pounced on a second wrapper a few feet away, half hidden under a mossy log. "Maybe he was dropping them to give us a way to follow him!"

Franny stopped looking cross and began to look scared. "We really should get Mom and Dad," she said.

"Let's just see if we can follow the trail a little farther," said Poppy. "Look, there's another one...."

Once they knew what they were looking for, it was easy to follow the trail of chocolate foil wrappers through the woods and right up to the base of a gnarled and massive oak tree that sat at the edge of the clearing.

Franny called out, "Rolly? Can you hear me?" She took a deep breath and yelled even more loudly, *"Roll-eeee!"*

Poppy's hand clapped over Franny's mouth.

"Shh, be quiet; do you want to let everyone know we're here?" Poppy hissed into her ear. "Let's fan out, see if we can find any more clues. The trail can't end here."

With a few more grumbles, Franny headed in one direction and Will in another. Poppy decided to climb the oak tree. From a higher vantage point, she reasoned, she might be able to spot something: a piece of clothing, a trampled section of grass, the glint of another chocolate wrapper. . . .

She easily swung herself up to a low branch, then settled down with her back to the trunk. She could hear Will thrashing through bushes to her left and faint squeals from Franny (who had undoubt-edly encountered another bug) to her right.

From her perch, she could see a thin branch on a nearby tree quiver as a squirrel ran along it. Other than that, there was little movement. It was a hot, breathless day. The leaves were still; the only sound was the faint hum of an airplane flying far overhead.

Out of the corner of her eye, she caught a small disturbance in the still, silent day. Carefully, she slewed her eyes to one side.

There. Trotting along the trail was a small gob-lin, wearing a pack on his back.

She sat up a little straighter and glanced toward where she had last seen Franny and Will. They were nowhere in sight. In fact, she couldn't even hear them anymore. And now the goblin had left the trail and was walking toward the big rock at the base of the oak tree.

He lowered his pack to the ground with a heavy sigh. Then he knocked three times on the rock. Poppy heard a deep groaning sound, then an opening appeared in the ground. The goblin picked up his pack and climbed down through the hole.

Before she even knew what she was doing, Poppy found that she had skinned down the tree and was on the ground. Two long strides took her to the rock.

She hesitated, wondering if she should call out to Will and Franny.

"I still don't know what we're doing out here...." Franny's voice was faint, but Poppy could hear the whining note clearly. "... I can't believe Poppy believes in goblins. ... I think she's been hanging out with Mom and Dad too much...."

Poppy gritted her teeth. She would show Will and Franny that she wasn't imagining things. She would prove to them that she knew what she was talking about. She knocked three times fast on the rock.

The ground disappeared, and she plummeted into darkness.

Chapter
FOURTEEN

Poppy fell too fast to be afraid. She landed on the ground with a thump that knocked the wind out of her lungs and every thought she had out of her brain. For what seemed like a very long time, she simply lay still on the ground and tried to remember how to breathe.

After a few seconds, she tried to yell for help, but only managed something that sounded like a breathy squeak. Above her head, she could hear Franny and Will yelling her name over and over like maniacs. Poppy felt a little pleased at the sound of panic in their voices, but this was overshadowed by the fact that they were making so much noise they couldn't hear her trying to get their attention.

She tried calling their names one or two more times, then decided to sit still and enjoy the ability to breathe for a while before trying again.

She pulled her mini-flashlight from her pocket and flicked it on. As she waved the beam around, she saw that she was in a cave about the size of the kitchen at home. It smelled dank and damp, and she could feel a cool breeze that seemed to come from somewhere deep underground.

She could see a faint area of lightness overhead and realized that was the hole she had fallen through. Her heart slowed down as she realized that she wasn't hurt and that it wouldn't be terribly difficult to get out—the rock wall seemed quite knobbly; she could probably find some footholds, enough to clamber up to the opening. Or, if worse came to worst, Will and Franny could go get a rope and pull her out.

Will and Franny's voices seemed to be drifting away.

"Hey!" she yelled. "I'm down here!"

"Poppy!" Will's voice came closer. "Where are

you?" Now he sounded as if he were right over her head.

She tried to warn him. "Will, stop! There's a—"

But it was too late. Will crashed through the hole and landed next to her.

"Oof," he said. "Ow."

"—hole in the ground," she finished, rather unnecessarily.

"Yes," he said. Even in the gloom, she could see that he was lying on his back and staring pensively up at the roof of the cave. "I noticed."

"What are you two think you're doing?" They both looked up to see Franny's face framed in the opening. She looked hot, sweaty, and very annoyed.

"First Poppy vanishes from sight and then Will decides to go charging through the bushes right after her," she went on. "You're both complete idiots, if you ask me."

"We're fine, thanks," Will said, glaring up at her.

"Now I suppose I'll have to go home and tell Mom and Dad, and they'll probably have to call a rescue squad to get you out of there." Franny started to straighten up. "Honestly, I don't know what you two would do without—"

Whatever she was about to say was lost as the ground near the edge of the hole gave way and Franny fell into the cave. Fortunately, her fall was broken, so she didn't land on the ground as Poppy and Will had. Unfortunately, her fall was broken by Will.

"Oof," he said. "Get . . . off . . . me. . . ."

Franny didn't move. "This is just great," she said, gazing bitterly at the small piece of blue sky she could see through the hole. "Just fantastic."

"Franny . . ." Will wheezed. His face was turning purple. ". . . *off* . . . me . . ."

"Now we're all trapped down here and there's no way out and no one knows where we've gone," she said in a musing voice. "Remind me. Whose brilliant plan was this?"

"Watch . . . out," Will managed to gasp. *"Spiders!"*

"What? Where?" Franny jumped to her feet

and began frantically brushing at her hair and clothes. "Are any of them on me?"

Instead of answering, Will closed his eyes and took in a deep shuddering breath.

"I think one crawled down my neck!" Franny pulled her shirt away from her body and shook it. "Will! Why didn't you say something?"

Will opened one eye enough to glare at her. "Oh, I don't know," he said. "Maybe it was because I couldn't talk because *someone was sitting on me!*" He raised himself on one elbow and looked around the cave. "What happened?"

"I think that's pretty obvious," said Poppy. "We fell through a hole in the ground."

Will frowned. "I didn't see any hole when we were in the clearing the other day—"

"Of course not," Poppy answered, feeling, in spite of her fear, a certain pride in having been proven right. "I saw a goblin on the trail, so I followed him. He knocked on the rock and the hole opened up, so I followed him and then I fell through the hole—"

"I can't believe it!" Franny thrust her hands

through her hair. "I can't *believe* we're stuck down here because of your goblin fixation."

"It's not a fixation—" Poppy began, but Franny turned her back on her and addressed Will.

"What do you think?" she asked. "Could we climb out of here somehow?"

Will stared at the hole in the cave ceiling, his eyes narrowed in thought. "Maybe," he said. "If I stood on your shoulders, I might be able to pull myself up there—"

Franny shot him a look. "Nice," she said. "Why don't *I* stand on *your* shoulders?"

"Because you weigh more than me," Will pointed out. "It only makes sense—"

Franny wheeled around. "Are you saying that I'm fat?" she asked dangerously.

"No, I'm just saying that there's a good chance that my knees might buckle and that you would drop to the ground like a stone," said Will.

"I can't believe you're saying that I'm fat!" Franny's eyes filled with tears. "I can't believe that my own brother—"

"Franny! Will!" Poppy snapped. "You're missing the point."

They both swung around to stare at her. "Forget about getting out of the cave! We have to rescue Rolly! He's been captured by goblins!"

"You keep saying that," said Will. "And we keep not believing you."

Poppy took a breath and counted to ten. "Look," she said, as calmly as she could. "Everything that's happened to us makes perfect sense. It's just like that book I was reading about the little people. There are all kinds of stories about people who followed a fairy through a door in the side of a hill and found themselves in another world—"

Franny stopped pacing long enough to give Poppy an accusing look. "I thought you said you saw a goblin."

"That's not the point! The point is that people have been telling stories for centuries about small creatures who live underground and only come out to make mischief for mortals," said Poppy. "Doesn't that sound like what's been happening to us?"

Will sighed and stared at the ground. Franny twirled a piece of hair around her finger and gazed up at the hole in the ceiling. Poppy stood still except for her tapping foot, mentally willing them to understand what she was saying, to accept what she had seen, to believe her.

"You know what you'd be saying if you were reading about this case in the PSI newsletter," Will said finally. "You'd lecture everybody about how all the things that have been going wrong at the house can be explained by natural causes, and about how people's eyes play tricks on them all the time, and how everyone sees what they want to see—"

"I would not!" said Poppy. She wasn't sure if she was more hurt by the fact that Will didn't believe her or by the fact that he said she was lecturing people when all she was really doing was reasonably pointing out certain logical flaws in their reasoning.

"Yes, you would, Poppy, and you know it," Franny joined in. "You're always telling people that extraordinary claims require extraordinary evidence. So where's your evidence?"

Poppy didn't answer. She was afraid that if she tried to speak, she might cry.

Instead, she turned her back on Will and Franny and began shining her flashlight across the walls of the cave. As it flickered across the back of the cave, it revealed a dark opening. She stood still for a long moment, staring into the darkness.

"That looks like a tunnel," she said finally. "I wonder where it goes?"

She didn't have to turn around to know that Will and Franny were exchanging wary glances. She could hear it in Will's voice when he said, "Don't be crazy, Poppy. First, let's figure out how to get out of here, then we'll tell Mom and Dad what's happened and let them find out where the tunnel goes. All right?"

Poppy began digging through her backpack. "I'm pretty sure I put some reflective tape in here," she said. "We can use that to make markers so we can find our way back out—"

"Poppy, for heaven's sake, you're supposed to be

the smart one!" Franny snapped. "What happens in every story about people who decide to explore a cave on a whim? They *die*, that's what happens."

"We won't go far," Poppy promised. She moved closer to the tunnel. As she did so, her flashlight's beam wandered across the dirt floor. It caught a dull gleam of tinfoil, wavered, and returned. Poppy reached down and picked up the candy wrapper and smoothed it open.

Another Choc-O-Bomb.

They stood in silence for what seemed like a long time. Poppy could hear the faint *drip, drip, drip* of water from somewhere deeper in the cave.

Then Franny said, in a trembling voice, "There's no way Rolly got down here on his own. He's too little."

"Exactly! That's what I've been *telling* you for the last three hours," said Poppy, holding on to her temper with an effort. "The goblins took him."

"Or he fell down here just like we did," Will pointed out.

"Fine. Forget the goblins, if that makes you feel

better," Poppy said. "We still have to get him back."

"On our own?" asked Will.

"In the dark?" asked Franny. "There might be spiders." She shuddered. "Or bats."

"Both, probably," said Poppy, rooting through her backpack again. "It *is* a cave. I brought an extra flashlight, just in case." She handed it to Will. "Here."

He took the flashlight in a halfhearted way. "I don't know if this is such a good idea. Franny's right. We should go get some help."

Poppy glared at him. "What if something happens to Rolly while we're gone?"

"What if something happens to *us*?" asked Will. "We don't even know for sure that Rolly's down here!"

"The candy wrapper—" Poppy began.

Will waved that aside. "Rolly's not the only person who eats Choc-O-Bombs. Someone else could have dropped it."

"That's right!" Franny said with relief. "Probably lots of people have explored this cave. It would be so stupid to get lost in this horrible cave just because you found some litter on the ground!"

Poppy chose to ignore this. "You two can stay here if you want," she said. "But I'm going after Rolly."

She started into the tunnel without even bothering to look back, her shoulders squared and her head held high. Maybe Will and Franny were too scared to go up against a gaggle of goblins, but *she* was made of sterner stuff. *She* wasn't going to let her little brother be spirited away by some pint-sized cave dwellers. And after she'd rescued Rolly and they had both returned safely home, *she* would be proven right and they would all have to admit that they had been completely and totally wrong—

"Poppy, wait!" said Will.

He grabbed her shoulder, making her flashlight beam slide across the cave wall.

"We don't have time—" Poppy had started to say when the flashlight suddenly revealed a goblin sticking out his tongue at her.

"Hey!" She jumped back, the flashlight beam

jerked to one side, and the face disappeared again into darkness. "Did you see that?"

"See what?" Franny asked.

"The goblin!"

Franny rolled her eyes. "If you're trying to scare us, Poppy, it's not working. And I personally think that's a very childish thing to do, especially at a time like this—"

Poppy wasn't listening. Carefully, she swept her flashlight back and forth across the rocky surface until—there! With an effort, she steadied her hand, then nodded toward the wall.

"Look," she said.

Will and Franny looked.

Amid the rocky outcroppings, half hidden in the shadows, was a small carving of a face. Its expression was impish. Its eyes were gleaming with mischief. And Poppy was quite sure that, if she could see its teeth, they would be pointed. That was impossible, however, for one simple reason: the goblin was sticking its tongue out at them.

Poppy couldn't help herself. She knew it was

childish and pointless, but still she found herself sticking out her tongue at the carving in return.

"What is that?" Franny squeaked.

"That," Poppy said with some satisfaction, "is a goblin. *Now* will you believe me?"

Chapter
FIFTEEN

"**I** think it's getting darker," Franny whispered. "Does it seem like it's getting darker to you? I mean, it was black before, but now it looks like a *blacker* black, don't you think?"

"Don't be ridiculous," Will snapped. "It's impossible to get darker than no light at all."

"And don't worry so much," Poppy said irritably. "We have extra flashlights and extra batteries, plus three candles and matches." She couldn't resist adding, somewhat smugly, "That's what comes of being prepared."

"I don't care what you say," Franny said, hugging herself. "It *is* getting darker! And we're probably surrounded by spiders. And it's getting colder, too. Remember what Mom told us about hypothermia that night we tramped all over the Yukon looking for Nuk-luk? We'll get colder and colder and then we'll feel sleepy and that's the last thing we'll ever know because we'll all be *dead*."

Sighing, Poppy stopped and took off her backpack. "No one's going to die of hypothermia," she said. "Here—"

She pulled out a sweater and tossed it to Franny, then handed a long-sleeved shirt to Will (nobly resisting the temptation to remind them how they had mocked her for packing extra clothes, back when they were all sweating in the Texas heat).

Poppy, of course, had put on a cardigan and a knit cap within moments of setting out to explore the cave. As she waited patiently for Will and Franny to pull on their extra clothes, she moved her flashlight over the rough walls and wondered exactly how long it would take someone to carve a face into that rock. . . .

A scuttling sound made them all jump.

"What was that?" Franny said, her voice shrill.

"Just some cave creature," said Poppy. Her heart was thumping wildly, but she tried to keep her voice even. "If I had to guess, I'd say it was a trogloxene, but it might have been a troglophile, I suppose—"

"What are you talking about?" Franny snapped.

"I'm talking about a cave's ecosystem," said Poppy, her heart gradually slowing down to a normal rhythm. Simply saying scientific words like *trogloxene* and *troglophile* made her feel calmer, more in control. It was what she loved about science—the idea that discovering facts and naming things could help you understand what was going on around you. "It just so happens that last month's issue of *Science Today* had a very interesting article about caves. Animals that can live either inside or outside a cave are called troglophiles, which means 'cave lovers.' That includes beetles, centipedes, snails, spiders—"

"I knew this cave felt all spidery," Franny muttered, brushing a hand nervously over her hair.

Poppy ignored this. "While trogloxenes, or cave

guests, are animals that live in caves but go outside at some point in their lives," she continued. "Everyone thinks of bats, but there are other creatures that come and go, like pack rats—"

"Of course there are," Franny said, her voice edged with hysteria. "Rats. Yes. We wouldn't want to forget the rats."

"Now troglobites, or cave dwellers, have to live their whole lives underground, so they become completely adapted to the dark." Despite their fraught circumstances, Poppy was beginning to enjoy herself. She did like sharing knowledge, even when her audience wasn't as receptive as she would have liked. "Actually, it's quite interesting how they adapt to constant darkness. There are sightless worms, fish with no eyes—"

"Okay, Poppy, you really have to stop talking now," said Franny, glaring at her. "Because I'm warning you, if I have to deal with blind worms *and* goblins, I'm going home right this second—"

"Hey," Will said. He was standing a few feet away, staring at the ground. "Look at this."

His flashlight beam was trained on a small gap between two rocks. Nestled in the gap was a Choc-O-Bomb candy wrapper.

"We can't turn back, Franny," Will whispered. "Poppy's right. We've got to keep going, no matter what."

As they kept walking, they gradually started talking more softly. Soon they found that they were moving closer together as they continued down the tunnel, occasionally even bumping into one another by accident.

When that happened, their flashlight beams would bounce crazily around the cave, sometimes startling them with strange sights, like a rock formation that (just for a second) they had all thought was a woman dressed in a long cloak, standing still and watching them, or a cluster of sleeping bats, hanging upside down from the ceiling.

Once in a while, a draft of cold, dank air would brush their faces, as if something large and unknown were moving deep inside the earth.

There were no sounds except water dripping and their own whispers.

Every time they had turned down a different tunnel, Poppy made a small pile of stones to mark the spot, then wrapped a piece of glow-in-the-dark tape around a Popsicle stick and stuck it in the pile. She also made Franny and Will turn around and look back the way they'd come.

"That's so we remember how it looks when we leave," she explained. "A lot of cave explorers get lost because they don't look back and can't recognize any landmarks."

Franny didn't find this explanation reassuring. "How do you know we won't get lost? We'll never find our way back; I don't care how many little signs you make!"

Still, as strange and otherworldly as the cave was, at least everything they saw and smelled and heard made a certain kind of sense.

At least, until they turned another corner and saw the wall of socks.

* * *

There were hundreds of them. They were hanging from the walls of the tunnel: brightly striped socks in blue, pink, red, green, and purple; dull men's socks in brown and black and navy; dainty white cotton socks with lace edging; tiny babies' socks; cartoony socks with popular TV characters or jaunty pictures of palm trees; dignified socks with tweed and herringbone patterns; lumpy knitted socks the color and texture of oatmeal; saucy red-mesh socks that fluttered in the slight breeze. . . .

The Malones stared, their flashlights moving back and forth over the display.

"You know," Will said finally, "this is really weird."

"Weird?" Franny's voice had developed a slightly hysterical edge. "Is that all you have to say? This is beyond weird, it's, it's . . ."

She stopped and threw up her hands, unable to find the right words to express how completely unexpected and strange this was.

"Like I said," said Will with some satisfaction. "Weird."

Poppy moved closer to the wall, playing her

flashlight over each sock in turn. "Look," she said. "Every single one is different. At least, I don't see any pairs, do you?"

"Who cares about whether there are pairs or not? We're not doing laundry, for heaven's sake," Franny said.

Poppy ignored this. "It might be a clue."

"To what?"

"I don't know; that's the whole point of a mystery," Poppy snapped. "Hey!" She pulled a red-and-white striped sock off the wall. "This is my sock. I was looking for it everywhere last week."

"Oh, well, that's just great," Franny said. "You lost a sock and now you've found it. Falling into a hole and getting lost in a cave and maybe dying will be completely worthwhile, now that you've completed your sock collection."

"Don't be an idiot, Franny," said Will. "Don't you see, this means something. . . ."

"Yes," said Poppy, stuffing the sock in her pocket. "The question is, what does it mean?" She swept her flashlight beam over the socks again.

"Who took these socks? Who put them on display? Why did they do it and what can we deduce from what we've found . . . ?"

"Aaggh." Franny groaned and clutched the sides of her head in what Poppy thought was an overly dramatic manner. "Enough already! Let's just find Rolly and get out of here!"

At that moment, Poppy heard a low, humming, gravelly sound in the distance.

"Shh," she said. "Listen."

The humming got closer.

"What is it?"

"I don't know," Will said. "We'd better hide."

He slipped behind a large boulder and Poppy followed.

"Come on," she said to Franny.

Franny glanced fearfully over her shoulder, then wrinkled her nose. "I'm not crawling back there. It's all slimy and gross and—"

"Hidden. Do you want to meet a goblin face-to-face?" Poppy grabbed her arm and pulled her sister behind the boulder.

223

Franny stepped on her toe, hard. Poppy bit her lip to keep from yelling and shifted toward Will. His elbow poked her in the ribs. With the three of them wedged into the narrow space, there was barely room to breathe.

"I don't know what you're making such a fuss about," said Franny.

"Shh!" Poppy and Will both said together.

She opened her mouth to say something else, but at that moment, a goblin came trudging down the tunnel, humming a dirgelike tune. A smaller goblin (Poppy thought she recognized the one who had turned the sprinklers on while her parents were dowsing) trotted along at his heels, carrying a glass jar.

"I wonder what we're going to have for dinner," the smaller goblin was saying. "I hope it's something good. Maybe we'll have baked eels or boiled parsnips or even fried worm cakes. What do you want to have for dinner?"

"Whatever Bother makes is fine with me," said the bigger goblin. "Do you suppose you could stop talking now, Muddle? Just for a minute or so? Just to please me?"

"Oh, sure, Glitch. No problem," said Muddle, nodding earnestly.

Two steps later, he stopped. "Oh, hey, wait! I forgot! I have a trophy to hang up—" He dropped his pack to the ground and began digging through it. "I know it's here somewhere. I remember putting it down at the bottom so I would be sure not to lose it. . . ."

"Can't we hang it later, Muddle?" Glitch asked. "I'm tired and hungry and ready to get out of these pustulous clothes—"

"No, look, I found it!" The smaller goblin bobbed back up, holding a dingy gray sock with pride. "See, I knew it wasn't lost."

"Great, fine, hang it up quickly so we can go home."

"But what about the ceremony?" Muddle asked. "This is the first sock I ever stole! And I almost got trapped inside the dryer, too! If I hadn't managed to wedge a dish towel in the door, I might have been captured!"

"Okay, okay, enough!" Glitch heaved a deep sigh, then said rapidly, "In recognition of his boldness and courage, in deep appreciation of his daring and cunning, we hereby allow the gremlin Muddle to hang his sock on the Wall of Valor, where it will remain in perpetuity as a tribute to the Goblin Spirit and our unwavering commitment to outwitting mortals, in every time and every place and every way that we can."

Muddle solemnly wedged a small stick in a crack in the stone and hung his sock from it, then stepped back and saluted.

Tapping his toes, Glitch paused for a few moments in what was obviously meant to be a reverent silence, then applauded in a perfunctory manner. "Very good," he said briskly. "Congratulations. Now let's *go*."

"Okay," said Muddle. He trotted along for several steps before adding, "I wonder what Mom will say when she sees all the fireflies I caught. I bet she'll be really happy, don't you? I bet she'll be impressed. What do you think?

Don't you think she'll be impressed—"

"Yes, yes, I'm sure she will." Glitch sighed. "I did tell you I had a headache, right?"

"Oh yeah, you did."

"And that it would be very nice to have some peace and quiet for a while? Even for just a little while?"

"Oh yeah, you said that."

"So do you think you manage it?"

"Manage what?"

There was a strange sound, almost as if Glitch were grinding his teeth. "Could you possibly manage to stop talking until we get home? If you weren't my own brother, I'd think you were part elf!"

"Well, I'm sorry," said Muddle. "I didn't know I was bothering you. I was just trying to make conversation. I was just trying to be friendly. But okay, fine. I won't say a word from now on. I'll just keep my mouth shut. You won't hear a single, solitary thing cross my lips for the rest of the night—"

They turned the corner, Muddle's voice gradually fading away as they walked out of sight.

Poppy cast a triumphant look at Franny and Will.

She was gratified to see that Franny's mouth had formed a perfect, astonished O and that Will's eyes were wide with disbelief.

"See?" she whispered. "What did I tell you? *Goblins.*"

"What a day I've had, Bother," Glitch said, striding over to the fire to warm his hands. "I was almost spotted again. It's getting worse and worse up there; nothing but mortals everywhere you look these days."

The Malones were huddled behind another boulder, peering through a windowlike opening into a small cave off the main tunnel. Poppy was fairly sure they had gone undetected. They had followed the goblins as quietly as they could. True, Franny had tripped more than once, and Will had been so eager to keep pace with their quarry that he had rounded a curve too quickly and had to dart backward when he saw the goblins only a

few feet away. Fortunately, Glitch had been showing Muddle how to detach a phosphorescent fungus
from the wall, and they had both been too absorbed
to notice Will.

Finally, the goblins had stopped. Safely hidden,
the Malones had seen Glitch open a small wooden
door and usher Muddle inside, calling out, "Hello,
Bother. We're home."

The door had closed behind them. Poppy sig-
naled to her brother and sister that they should
wait before making a move. As her eyes adjusted to
the dark, she could see a carving next to the door.
Like the one at the cave's entrance, the carving por-
trayed a goblin's head, but the goblin was grinning
a wide grin that showed off all his pointed teeth.

Poppy studied it for a few moments. Why, she
wondered, did goblins need such very sharp teeth?
What did they use them for? They looked very
much like the kind of teeth one would see on a
vicious predator—a bear, say, or a shark. . . .

Before her thoughts could travel any further
along these unwelcome lines, Poppy motioned to

Will and Franny. Together, they crept up to the door, which was flanked on both sides by rough-cut openings that served as windows.

When they peeked in, they saw a cozy room aglow with light. A half-dozen hurricane lamps were placed on shelves and small tables, while a fire crackled in a large hearth. Several chairs, each one plump with cushions and covered with dark velvet, were clustered in front of the fire. To the left was a long wooden table lined with trays of cookies. Even from a distance, Poppy could smell sugar and cinnamon and some strange spice that she couldn't identify.

Another goblin was tending to several pots that bubbled on top of an iron stove; when she opened the stove door, the aroma of fresh-baked bread wafted through the air, making Poppy's stomach growl with hunger.

"It must be dreadful, dear," the goblin said, calmly stirring the stew. "But you're both back safe; that's all that matters. Did you manage to pick up any batteries while you were Above Ground?"

"I did!" Muddle said proudly, reaching into his pocket. He pulled out a handful of batteries and held them up for her inspection. "I lifted six of them!"

The goblin beamed at him. "That's wonderful, Muddle. You're turning into quite the scavenger, aren't you? I wouldn't be surprised if you graduated to goblin within the year."

Muddle looked gratified by this praise. "Look what else I brought back," he said, holding up the cage of insects. "Forty-two lightning bugs! That's a new record! Last week Blister caught forty lightning bugs and he was bragging about it, but I knew I could do better and I did! I got forty-two! That's two more than Blister, because he only got forty—"

"Yes, dear, very nice. You are coming along quite nicely." She put the batteries into a small lava lamp, then switched it on. She smiled as red and orange bubbles began hypnotically rising and falling. "Oh, that *is* nice. It's good to have the lamp turned on again. I think it makes the kitchen look so cheery, don't you?"

"Uh-huh." Muddle snuck a cookie off the tray.

"Stop that." She slapped his hand playfully. "Dinner's almost ready."

"You know, Glitch didn't get any batteries, and when he tried to catch a firefly he fell in the creek," said Muddle. "You should have heard what he said! Do you want to hear what he said? Because I memorized all the words so that I could tell you what he said." He stopped to take a breath. "Glitch wouldn't tell me what some of the words mean, so I thought I would ask you. Do you want me to tell you what he said now?"

"That won't be necessary," she said. "Go and wash your hands for dinner."

He opened his mouth to protest and she gave him a stern look. "Now."

When he left the room, Glitch gave her a martyred glance. "You see what I have to put up with," he said. "I believe I might be going mad."

"I know that training gremlins is hard, but you're doing a wonderful job with him," she said, setting a bowl of stew on the table.

"It gets in the way of my own work, though," Glitch said. "Like today. I had to stand absolutely still for almost half an hour while some silly woman pruned her roses. And a bee landed on my nose! I was in mortal fear the whole time that it would figure out I wasn't made out of ceramic and sting me!"

"Dear, dear," she said absently, clucking her tongue. "That sounds dreadful. Come here and taste this stew—do you think it has enough salt?"

"It *was* dreadful! In fact, it was a complete nightmare! Not to mention that Muddle can't seem to learn how to break a guitar string or scare a cat, no matter how much I work with him. And after all that, what do I have to show for today's work! Just this!"

He reached into his coat and pulled out a round lid from a plastic food storage container.

"Well, at least you came back with something," she said soothingly. She took it from him and held it up in front of the fire, turning it this way and that in order to admire it. "What a nice shade of blue! This will be a lovely addition to my collection. Thank you, dear."

"That's all right," he said. "Glad you like it."

She opened a cupboard door to reveal stacks of plastic lids in all shapes and sizes. "I just wish I could be Above Ground to hear what those mortals say tonight when they're putting away their leftovers."

Glitch snickered at the thought.

"'Now, where is the lid for this container?'" she went on, imitating the puzzled owner of the missing lid. "'I know I put it in the cupboard just yesterday! I swear, they just seem to disappear on their own sometimes!'"

Glitch laughed, then stretched his arms above his head, and tilted his head back and forth to work out a crick in his neck. "Ah, it's good to be home."

He took off his long red cap and tossed it on a small table, followed by his white beard, then his jacket (which had clearly been padded, since his round belly disappeared as well).

He made a face at each item as he pulled it

off and muttered, "I absolutely loathe wearing camouflage."

"I know, dear, so horrible. I don't know how you stand it," Bother said absently. "Why don't you get changed for dinner?"

Glitch disappeared through a dark doorway and returned a few moments later looking transformed. He had brushed the white powder from his hair, revealing a mop of dark curls, and washed his face, scrubbing away his rosy cheeks. He looked altogether slimmer, younger, and more elegant.

"Sit down," she said. "Your dinner's getting cold." She turned to call through the door. "Muddle! It's time for dinner!"

"Ah! That smells good." He settled into one of the chairs and gratefully dipped his spoon into the stew.

She poured a cherry-red liquid into two glasses and handed one to Glitch. He raised his glass to her.

"A toast," he said, grinning. "To Treasure and Trouble!"

His drink was halfway to his mouth when Franny sneezed.

The Malones froze. Glitch's eyes swung to the window, narrowing in suspicion. Before they could even think about running, he had crossed the room, flung open the door, and was standing in front of them, his hands on his hips.

"Oh, wonderful," he said in disgust. "This is all I need after a day like today. Well, don't just lurk around in the dark. Come inside and let us take a look at you."

Slowly and reluctantly, Poppy, Will, and Franny stepped forward into the light.

Chapter
SIXTEEN

"**O**h no, not *more* humans!" said Bother. She glared accusingly at Glitch. "Really, this is too much! Where in the world are we going to put them all?"

"*I* don't know," he snapped. "I didn't invite them here, you know. They just showed up."

Together, the two goblins turned to stare at their unexpected guests with equal parts curiosity and worry. Only Muddle seemed happy at the turn of events. His face was shining with delight.

"Can we keep them?" he asked eagerly.

"No, we cannot!" said Bother.

"*Please?*" he asked. "I'll take care of them, I promise."

"You say that now, but we all know who will end up feeding them and taking them for walks," said Bother, still staring at the three children standing in front of her.

They stared back at her. Suddenly, Franny's eyes narrowed. She leaned down to look more closely at Bother's ears. A silver heart dangled from her right ear and a fake diamond glittered on her left ear.

"Hey!" Franny said. "Those are my earrings! I was looking for them everywhere yesterday!"

Bother took a nervous step back, her hands cupped protectively over her ears. "I wouldn't know about that," she said vaguely. "Actually, they were a gift—"

"I can't believe it," Franny said. She turned an outraged face to Poppy. "That goblin stole my earrings!"

"That's what I've been trying to tell you," said Poppy. "All the lost keys and spilled sugar and blown fuses—they're behind everything that's been going wrong at our house."

"Well, I think it's very childish," Franny said.

"Annoying people for no good reason!"

Bother snorted. "Oh, we've got a very good reason," she said. "If you want to talk about mischief, just take a look at what you mortals get up to. Always starting a war or building a shopping mall or inventing something horrible, like fluorescent lighting—"

"Okay, okay." Will sighed. "We get it!"

"Just think what you'd manage to do if you didn't spend half your lives looking for socks or searching for keys," Bother said. "If it weren't for goblins, the world wouldn't be worth living in."

"Excuse me," Poppy said. "This is all very interesting, but I think we're losing track of the main point here—"

"And now we've got three more of you horrible creatures down here!" Bother shot an exasperated look at Glitch. "Whatever happened to the warding you placed on the portal?"

Glitch ran his hands through his hair. "Muddle and I had to open it when we returned from scavenging. They must have slipped in right behind us."

He scowled at the Malones, adding bitterly, "They just happened to be in the right place at the right time, and now *we* have to deal with them. What a mess!"

"It's not our fault," Franny said indignantly. "We didn't ask you to kidnap Rolly."

"We'd be glad to leave right now," said Will.

"Wait, don't tell me," Glitch said, holding up a hand. He pretended to think for a moment, then snapped his fingers. "I know!" he said. "You've come to rescue your little brother! No, no, don't try to deny it. I've seen that expression of heroic valor before."

"We're not denying anything," Poppy snapped. "Of course we're here to get him back."

"And how, I wonder, are you going to do that?" Glitch asked. "Even supposing you could find your way out of our caves, what makes you think we'd let you take Rolly with you? We went to quite a lot of trouble to get him, you know."

Poppy shuddered. Part of her wanted to ask exactly why the goblins had gone to so much trouble to get Rolly; part of her was afraid to find out.

"If you don't let us take him, we'll get help," Will threatened.

"Yes!" Franny said. "We'll tell our parents! We'll tell the police!"

Glitch and Muddle snickered. Even Bother bit her lip as if trying not to laugh.

"What?" Franny said, her face reddening. "What's so funny?"

"And what will the police do when you tell them that goblins have stolen your brother?" asked Glitch. "If they take you seriously, which I doubt, they'll go to your house. And what will they find? Your parents, who don't know what you're talking about. Your brother, alive and well and looking exactly the same as always. And you three. Children with perhaps too much imagination for their own good."

The Malones could think of nothing to say to this.

"Now, now, don't look so upset," Bother said. "We've been stealing mortal children for a long, long time, you know. It makes sense that we'd be quite good at it."

"Well, I think that's terrible!" said Franny. "I don't know how you can brag about kidnapping a sweet little boy like Rolly away from his family who loves him!"

This would have been a more touching speech, Poppy thought, if Franny hadn't delivered it in such a throbbing voice. She sounded as if she were auditioning for a part in a play.

Apparently, Glitch thought much the same thing. "How very touching," he said in a sarcastic drawl. "So. You've decided that you like your little brother after all."

"Of course we do!" Franny said, raising the level of anguished grief another notch or two. "We *love* him!"

"I'm only asking," Glitch continued, "because I seem to remember hearing someone"—he looked pointedly at Franny—"calling him a pest."

"I didn't mean it," mumbled Franny, who began studying the toes of her sneakers with fierce concentration.

"And I think I heard someone else"—Glitch

turned his small glittering eyes to Will— "complaining about how Rolly has complicated all your lives."

"Well, he has," Will said stubbornly. He paused, then added, "I didn't mean it in a *bad* way."

Shifting his gaze to Poppy, Glitch went on relentlessly, "And I'm almost certain I heard some other person saying that perhaps you should have left him in the woods to find his way home."

"It was just a joke," she said weakly.

Glitch shrugged. "Nonetheless," he said. "Your wishes were heard and your wishes were answered—"

"Don't try to blame us for this," Poppy snapped. "Fine, we complained about Rolly. We didn't ask you to kidnap him!"

Glitch pursed his mouth at this, but finally nodded. "True enough," he said. "All the same, you have nothing to complain about now, especially since you still have a brother, a very nice one, as a matter of fact." He smoothed his ruffled shirt complacently. "Much better than the one you had before."

"We don't want a better brother," Poppy said. "We want Rolly."

"Do you, indeed?" Glitch's pointed white teeth flashed in the firelight. "Well, then. Let me take you to him."

They set off within minutes, after Glitch and Bother had managed to settle Muddle, who had badly wanted to go with them.

"Please?" he had whined. "Pleeease? I want to play with Rolly. Pleasepleasepleaseplease*please*!"

Bother had raised an eyebrow and pointed to the small wooden chair by the hearth. "Time to do your homework, Muddle," she said sternly. "You can't play with Rolly every minute of the day, after all."

Muddle had grumbled and complained, but he had finally sat down in the chair and pulled a reel of fishing line from his pocket. Muttering under his breath, he had started to tangle the line; within seconds, he had created a snarled mess.

"That's right," Bother had said proudly. "Just

keep it at it, Muddle, and you'll be the youngest gremlin allowed to go on a trip Above Ground all on your own."

Muddle still looked a bit disgruntled, but he had settled down to his tangling with a resigned air. Glitch then led Poppy, Will, and Franny out the door, farther along the tunnel they had previously traveled, and then right into a smaller side tunnel. The darkness, as soon as they were five steps away from the welcoming light of the goblins' home, seemed deeper than ever. Glitch held a long pole with a cage dangling from the end. The cage was filled with fireflies, which cast a flickering green light on the stone as he led them through a series of twisting tunnels.

"Step lively now," he called over his shoulder. "You wouldn't want to be left behind. Not down here in the cold and the dark."

As they followed Glitch deeper into the cave, the air seemed to get colder with every step, as if they were walking down into a place where it was always winter. It was hard to believe that they had left a blazing hot summer day just a short time ago, or that it still existed somewhere up above them.

Poppy slowed her pace a bit until the others had moved several yards in front of her. Carefully, she took off her backpack, reached inside, and pulled out a small sack of her father's Roman coins, grateful for the impulse that had made her dash back to the house and take them from his study. She wasn't even sure why she had taken them—vague ideas of bribing the goblins had run through her mind—but now, as she left one near the tunnel wall, she thought they would come in quite handy. She was concentrating on memorizing every turn they took, of course, but it wouldn't hurt to leave a little trail behind. . . .

As they followed Glitch, they occasionally passed several small wooden doors. Poppy eyed them, wondering where they led. They looked similar to the entrance to Glitch's home; like Glitch's door, each one had a goblin head carved into the rock next to it. Maybe the cave was filled with little goblin houses, she thought. Or maybe—her pulse quickened—maybe the doors led to other tunnels or secret passages. Maybe one of those doors could lead them back to the surface and back to freedom. . . .

Of course, Poppy thought, her spirits sinking, tunnels or passages could lead up or down. They could be built to connect different parts of the cave or created to confuse unwelcome visitors.

Poppy scowled at the carvings as she walked past, then glanced at Glitch, strutting along in front of Will and Franny. The firefly cage swung to one side, casting shadows on his face. For a second, he looked exactly like one of the stone carvings, although his expression was far more smug than any she had seen so far.

He thinks he's caught us, she thought. He thinks he's smarter than we are. Well, we'll see about that. . . .

Poppy eased another coin out of her pocket, then stopped and pretended to tie her shoe. She tucked the coin into a crevice between two rocks, then stood up and checked that she'd be able to spot it later.

She hurried to join the others before Glitch noticed that she was lagging behind. Unfortunately, she was so intent on catching up with them that she almost ran into Franny, who was tiptoeing cautiously around a large puddle in the middle of the tunnel.

"Watch where you're going!" Franny spat.

"Sorry," whispered Poppy.

"You should be!" said Franny. "It's your fault that we're going to be trapped down here! Trapped *forever*. In a *cave*. With *goblins*."

"Don't worry," said Poppy. "I have a plan."

"Oh, great. You have a plan," Franny said sarcastically. "It was your plan that landed us here. Trapped *forever*. In a *cave*. With *gob*—"

"Shh!" Poppy pinched Franny.

Franny yelped.

Glitch stopped. "What's going on back there?" he demanded.

Franny and Poppy looked at him with wide, innocent eyes. "Nothing," they chorused.

The goblin grinned at them. "Glad to hear it," he said. "We wouldn't want any mischief, now would we?"

"Of course not," said Poppy.

"All right, then." He smirked at her, then turned back around and started moving at a faster trot. "Let's get going."

Poppy looked at Franny and raised one eyebrow. Franny looked at Poppy and rolled her eyes.

"Sorry," Poppy whispered. "But I do have a plan. Trust me."

And she reached into her pocket for another coin.

They had walked for another fifteen minutes according to the luminescent dial of Poppy's watch before they turned one last corner and stopped, their eyes momentarily too dazzled to see.

Poppy blinked. They were standing at the edge of a cavern that glowed with light. Throughout the room, guttering candles had been placed on boulders or set in candlabras. Dozens of small niches—each one holding a candle or small oil lamp—had been carved in the stone walls. The flickering light went up at least two stories before the walls disappeared into the darkness.

"Welcome," Glitch said, "to Goblin Hall."

Poppy heard a stifled laugh somewhere to her left. She jerked her head around, but saw nothing but candlelight reflected in glistening rock walls.

"What was that?" she asked sharply.

Glitch stopped and turned to smile his pointed white smile at her. "What was what?" he asked, his black eyes gleaming with amusement.

He's laughing at me, she thought, and raised her chin a haughty half-inch. "Nothing," she said. "Where's Rolly?"

"All in good time," Glitch said. "All in good time."

The cavern was filled with shadows, which shifted and fluttered in the flickering light. She thought she saw something scuttle along the wall, but when she turned her head, she saw nothing except several large boulders and another iron-banded door.

She turned again, but it—whatever *it* was— was already gone.

Still, she seemed to catch glimpses out of the corner of her eye of something—something more than shadows—moving about, just on the edge of her vision. And yet, every time she turned her head to see *what* was moving, she found herself facing nothing but rocks, boulders, and a stone wall.

Poppy suddenly remembered a night when she was seven years old. She, Franny, and Will had been sent to stay at her grandmother's house during a summer when her parents had traveled to South America to track the mysterious and elusive Mono Grande. She had gone to bed on that first night, tired and ready to fall asleep. But when she had turned out the light, she had seen it: a witch, lurking in the corner of her room, ready to pounce on her as soon as her eyes drifted closed. . . .

Poppy could still recall with perfect clarity how she had lain straight and still in her bed, afraid that the slightest movement would let the witch know that *she* knew that the witch was there. She had tried to calm herself by listing all the reasons why witches didn't exist or, if they did, why it was impossible for one to be in her room. It didn't work. No matter what she told herself, she could see the wicked profile, the pointed hat, the long black cloak. . . .

Then her grandmother had opened the door to say good night. Soft light had spilled in from the hall, and Poppy had seen that the witch was nothing but a coat hanging on the back of a closet door.

Poppy felt a wave of relief at the memory.

Then she saw a shadow detach itself from one of the boulders.

Poppy's heart lurched in her chest as the shadow slipped along the wall and out of sight.

"Everything all right there?" Glitch asked slyly.

She turned to see him watching her closely, one eyebrow raised in a very irritating manner.

"Fine," she said coolly. "Except that I still don't see my little brother—"

Before she could finish, Muddle burst through one of the doors and ran toward them.

"Hi again!" he said, grinning cheerfully. "I know you said I couldn't come with you, but I kept asking and asking and asking and Bother finally said, 'Okay, okay, just *go*,' so here I am—"

"Pschwaz!" Glitch's eyes widened with alarm as a draft of air swept through the open door.

Muddle stopped in his headlong rush, his mouth hanging open in dismay. "Oops."

For a long, tense moment, Glitch and Muddle stared as the candles sputtered dangerously in the breeze. Poppy had just noticed how the leaping light made the goblin carving seem almost alive, when several candles and all the oil lamps went out completely.

A low murmur swept through the cave.

Poppy cocked her head to one side. It sounded vaguely like voices, but definitely not human ones, and there was a throbbing sense of . . . what? Worry, she thought finally. Dread. Maybe even fear . . .

Glitch ran over to the door, slammed it shut, then stood still, clearly holding his breath. Poppy just had time to notice how odd it was to see the goblin carving above Glitch's head sticking out its tongue gleefully while Glitch's face looked so tense and worried, and then the air stilled, the flames steadied, and the candles burned brightly once more.

Glitch's shoulders slumped with relief, then he turned furiously on Muddle.

"What in the name of all that's maggoty would make you come through a door like that?" Glitch asked sharply. "What were you *thinking*?"

"I'm sorry," Muddle said, his face crumpling. "I just wanted to see Rolly again."

"You and the rest of the known world," grumbled Glitch. "All right, all right. Come with me, then."

He stomped across the cavern with Poppy, Will, and Franny close behind. Without pausing, he flung open a door.

It wasn't hard for Poppy to peer over Glitch's shoulder, since he was only two feet tall. She had a clear view of Rolly standing in the middle of a bare stone room, blinking in the sudden light. He looked small and lonely and even—unwelcome tears pricked Poppy's eyes—ever so slightly scared.

Franny, of course, took full advantage of the moment. She pushed past Glitch and rushed over to kneel by Rolly, throwing her arms around him and clutching him tightly. "Oh, thank goodness we finally found you, Rolly!" she declaimed. "Don't be scared—we're here to rescue you!"

But Rolly merely pulled himself out of her grasp and scowled at them all. "What took you so long?"

Chapter
SEVENTEEN

"**W**e came as fast as we could, you ungrateful little brat," Franny said, abandoning all attempts to stage a heartwarming family reunion. She stood up, dusted off her knees, and looked around. "What is this place? Some kind of dungeon?"

Poppy winced. Will rolled his eyes. Too late, Franny caught herself.

"Sorry," she said to Glitch. "But it does look like you could use a few decorating tips."

"Well, who knows, maybe you'll be here long enough to transform the place," said Glitch. "In the meantime, feel free to settle in, make yourselves comfortable, let us know if you need anything." He cackled at the thought. "I'll be back soon—just as soon as we figure out what we're going to do with all of you."

As soon as Glitch and Muddle had gone, closing the door behind them, Poppy turned to survey the room. A small metal brazier sat in one corner, emitting belches of smoke and a faint warmth that did little to dispel the chill in the air. A few thin mattresses were stacked in another corner, along with blankets and pillows.

One small mattress had been placed in front of the brazier, and a rumpled blanket and pillow had been laid crookedly on top of it. Clearly, this was where Rolly had been sleeping.

The sight of the little bed—and the fact that Rolly had tried to make it—made her throat feel tight. She decided to risk giving him a hug.

"What are you *doing*?" He twisted away from her, his face red. "Stop it! Why does everyone keep hugging me?"

"It's just that we're glad to see you," Poppy said, a little hurt but not really surprised; Rolly had never been much of a hugger.

He eyed her suspiciously. "You are?"

"Sure," Will said. "We thought we might never find you again."

Rolly stared at Will. "So what? You have Blot now. I bet you like him better than me anyway."

Will and Franny looked at each other blankly.

"Blot?" Franny said. "Who's Blot?"

"The changeling, of course," Poppy said impatiently. "The goblin who took Rolly's place."

Rolly's lower lip jutted out. "You probably didn't even notice I was gone," he said. "You probably didn't miss me at all."

"Well, he does look a lot like you—" Will began.

Poppy raised her eyebrows. He shut his mouth with a snap. Rolly's frown deepened into the stubborn, mulish look they knew all too well and he said, "Maybe I won't ever come home. Maybe I'll stay down here where people like me."

"Oh, *please*," Franny said with a flip of her hand. "Live the rest of your life with goblins? I don't think so."

"Listen, Rolly," Poppy said, giving her sister a quelling look, "we knew right away that something was wrong. And we didn't like Blot at all." She knelt down so she could look into Rolly's eyes. "Oh, he was nice enough, I suppose, but having him around just wasn't the same. He wasn't *you*."

Rolly furrowed his brow as he thought that over. Finally, he said, "You didn't like him? Even though the goblins taught him to be nice all the time and mind his manners and never get into trouble?"

Poppy gave Will a meaningful look over Rolly's shoulder, and Will picked up his cue as if they'd rehearsed it.

"That was the whole problem!" Will said. "That little goblin was completely boring."

"He was?" Rolly asked.

"Yep." Will nodded. "He never once tried to fill the bathtub with Jell-O or trained ants to march across the kitchen floor. Remember when you did that, Rolly?"

Rolly didn't quite smile, but a contented,

remembering look appeared on his face. "Uh-huh."

"And remember when you tied a rope to the ceiling fan to see if you could hang on long enough to fly?" Poppy said. "Now *that* was an innovative idea. And very entertaining, too. Especially when you crashed into the bookshelf."

Rolly's nose twitched slightly. "Dad didn't think so," he pointed out.

"Geniuses always go unrecognized by their parents," Poppy assured him. "But now that we've had to live with . . . What's his name?"

"Blot," Rolly said darkly.

"Now we realize how much we liked having you around," Poppy said. "Blot's just not interesting. Not interesting at all."

Franny's mouth was hanging open slightly in disbelief as she stared at Poppy and Will. "What are you two talking about? Rolly's the reason I can't ever invite friends to the house—ow!"

She rubbed her ankle, staring resentfully at Poppy.

"Exactly," Poppy said quickly. "And I bet the

people in Emporia are still talking about that Fourth of July party, right, Franny?"

A few beats late, Franny finally caught on. "Oh, er, yes," she said. "Everyone who's ever crossed paths with you is still talking about it, Rolly. Mrs. Wilson—remember, that lady who lived next to us in Akron?—she still e-mails Mom for updates to see how you're doing."

"And to make sure you don't ever come within fifty miles of her house," Will muttered under his breath.

"Please, Rolly," said Poppy. She put as much urgency into her voice as she could. "It's not the same without you. We really, really want you to come home."

Rolly thought it over for five seconds, then nodded.

"Okay," he said. "Let's go."

"There's just one slight problem," said Franny. She nodded toward the wooden door with its heavy iron latch. "How are we going to get out?"

Poppy grinned, stepped over Rolly's makeshift

bed, and lifted the latch with one finger. The door swung open smoothly, revealing a tantalizing glimpse of the empty tunnel outside.

"I was watching Glitch when he left us here, just in case I would notice something that would help us get out," she said triumphantly. "And guess what? He forgot to lock the door! Now all we have to do is sneak away before he comes back and we'll be home before anyone notices that we're gone."

"Nice," Franny said approvingly.

But Will just shook his head. "Glitch didn't forget anything. He didn't lock the door because he doesn't have to. There's no way we'll ever find our way out of this place."

"That's where you're wrong, Will." Poppy tried not to look smug as she pulled the last Roman coin from her pocket and held it, shining on her palm in the candlelight. "I already thought of that. Come on."

The goblin laughter didn't start for at least ten minutes. Poppy would later remember those ten minutes fondly. Her plan was working: the goblins had been outsmarted, and they were on their way home. She even allowed herself to enjoy a daydream in which Glitch discovered they were gone, turned purple with rage, and gave a ringing speech about how deluded he had been, thinking that he could get the best of someone as clever and intrepid as Poppy Malone.

If they weren't trying to move as quietly as possible, Poppy would have started humming. Instead, she held firmly to Rolly with one hand and moved her flashlight beam back and forth across the ground with the other. Every time the flashlight picked up a flash of gold, she pocketed another coin with the happy thought that they were a few steps closer to getting out of the cave and going home.

Poppy couldn't hear anything except the faint drip of water from the rock over their heads and the quiet sound of her own breathing. Then, faint but ominously clear, a sound of scurrying and a rattle of pebbles, as if someone—or something— had run by in the dark.

Franny gave a squeak of dismay. "I really, really, *really* hope that was just a rat."

Someone chuckled.

It was a soft, delighted laugh. In other circumstances—say, if they were back home, sitting on the porch, sipping lemonade and enjoying a beautiful day—it would have merely sounded amused. But down here, where even the slightest sound echoed weirdly from the rock walls, it took on a much more sinister tone.

"That didn't *sound* like a rat," said Will.

"How do you know?" asked Franny, rather shrilly. "Maybe that's how rats sound when they're on their own."

"Gee, that's an interesting theory," he said. "When human eyes can't see them, the rats of the world sit around telling each other rat jokes and playing rat games and laughing little rat laughs—"

"Shh." Poppy held up a hand to silence them. "Listen."

They all held their breath. There was a tapping sound from behind them—*tap, tap, tap*—but when

Poppy turned her flashlight in that direction, she saw nothing except a large, furry spider scuttling behind a rock. Franny whimpered.

The tapping started up again, a little louder this time and once more from behind them. Poppy swung around again. Again, the light beam revealed nothing except a stalagmite stretching toward the ceiling of the cave. Or had she seen the stalagmite's shadow slip away to the left?

Poppy flicked her flashlight in that direction— and a goblin suddenly loomed at them out of the dark. She jumped, the flashlight beam skittered away, and the goblin disappeared once more.

"What was that?" Will yelled.

Poppy swept her flashlight back and forth until she caught a glimpse of the goblin's face again.

"It's just another carving," she said with relief. She walked over to examine it more closely. It stuck its tongue out at her. Scowling, she stuck her tongue out in response, thinking that, of all the expressions she'd seen so far, this one was her least favorite.

"I've read about people finding petroglyphs

in caves, but they're usually just carved lines or maybe a rough image of some sort," she said, half to herself. "I don't think I've ever come across any mention of carvings like these—"

"Poppy." Franny's voice was tight. "Do you think you could interrupt the lecture long enough for us to *get out of here*?"

"Wait just a minute. . . ." Poppy moved closer to the carving and leaned in until she was almost nose to nose with it. Something teased at the back of her mind, a vague idea that she couldn't quite capture. It had something to do with the goblin's expression, the way he seemed to be mocking her, as if he had a secret.

And yet, she had the sense that the clue to that secret was right in front of her, if only she could figure it out. . . .

"Come on." Even Will sounded a little nervous. "We don't know when Glitch might come back to check on us and find out we're gone."

Whatever brilliant thought Poppy was about to have vanished.

"Thanks a lot, Will," she snapped. "I was just about to have a blinding scientific insight, but now it's gone—"

It was when she tried to turn around that she discovered that something seemed to have gone wrong with her legs. Her right foot moved three inches, then stopped. She teetered for a moment as her brain tried to figure out what was wrong . . .

. . . and then she promptly fell flat on her stomach.

"Hey, are you okay—" Will's question ended in a grunt as he, too, crashed to the ground.

"For heaven's sake, what's wrong—oh!" Within one step, Franny, too, fell down.

The cave erupted in sniggering goblin laughter.

Poppy sat up and looked around wildly, but there were no goblins to be seen. Just shifting shadows and the echo of that jeering laughter.

"Stop it!" she shouted.

To her amazement, the laughter stopped. The back of Poppy's neck prickled.

She grabbed her flashlight and pointed it at her

feet. Her shoelaces had been tied together—tied so thoroughly, in fact, that they were now a tight tangle of knots. The same prank, she saw, had also been played on Will and Franny. Only Rolly was still standing.

He trotted over to where Poppy, Franny, and Will were sprawled in the dirt and stood smiling down at them.

"I could have told you not to wear those kind of shoes around goblins," he said smugly. He pointed to his own shoes, which fastened with a Velcro strap. "See? You should wear sneakers like mine. Goblins hate these kind of shoes."

"So does everyone over the age of five," Franny muttered as she tried to untie her shoes. "How did those goblins follow us without us seeing them, anyway?"

Poppy stopped tugging at her laces. "That's a good question," she said thoughtfully.

"And how did they mess with our shoes without us noticing?" asked Will.

"They're very clever," Rolly said. "That's why

they asked me to live with them, because they said that *I* am very clever, too. More clever than any other mortal they've ever seen. That's what they said."

"Oh, is that so?" snapped Will, whose efforts to unknot his laces had come to nothing. "And what made them think *you're* so smart?"

Rolly stared at him. "They watched me," he said.

Poppy felt a chill. The memory of Glitch staring at Rolly as he spread peanut butter on a window screen flashed through her mind. "They love to play pranks on humans," she said slowly. "Maybe they thought that all the, well, *unusual* things that Rolly does—"

"You mean the crazy things he does," Franny said bluntly. She blew a wisp of hair out of her face, then bent over her shoes again.

"They said I was a natural," Rolly said. "They said I had a talent for troublemaking."

"A talent?" Will scoffed. "You're an absolute *genius*." He gave a particularly vicious yank to one of the knots and managed to rip his shoes without, however, actually untangling his laces.

"Well, that's just great." He examined his torn sneakers with disgust. "These cost me all my Christmas and birthday money last year."

"I told you not to spend it all on one thing," Franny said primly. "I told you you were being a spendthrift."

Will gave her a murderous look, but settled for simply reaching down to pull off his shoes. "Forget it. I'll walk out of here in my socks."

"You don't have to do that." Rolly trotted over to Will and plucked at his shoelaces with small, delicate movements. Within moments, the snarls had disappeared.

Poppy's mouth dropped open. "How did you do that?"

Rolly shrugged. "I don't know."

"We always knew he had powers," Will said, happily retying his shoes. "We just didn't know that he could use them for good as well as evil."

"No, really," Poppy insisted. "I want to know—"

"Oh, for heaven's sake!" Franny cried. "Who cares?" She thrust her feet at Rolly. "Can you do mine next? Please?"

"We have to move faster," Poppy said. "I dropped ten coins and we've found five. That means we're halfway home."

But the goblins had other ideas.

A few minutes later, Franny spotted a coin and picked it up, only to find that it was smeared with something sticky.

"Aaggh!" She dropped the coin and automatically wiped her hand on her shorts before realizing what she was doing.

"Oh no!" she wailed. "My new shorts!"

A goblin chuckle echoed through the tunnel.

Franny whirled around. "This is not funny!" she shouted, too angry now to be scared. "I spent a month's allowance on these shorts!"

"A month's allowance," Will muttered. "And she calls *me* a spendthrift."

"These are *designer* shorts," she responded

huffily. "*Movie stars* wear them. I saw a photo in a magazine—"

"Forget it," Poppy said. "Just throw them in the washer when we get home."

"I can't do that; they're *linen*," Franny snapped. "And you know that if I take them to the dry cleaners, they'll tell me they can't get the stains out; they *always* do—"

"Franny." Poppy grabbed her arm. "Focus. Laundry is not our biggest problem right now."

"Yeah, quit acting like such a princess," said Will. "Just pick up the coin and let's keep going."

Franny tossed her head. "I'm not touching that," she said, her lip curling with disdain. "It's all sticky and dirty and gross."

"I will," Rolly said, pocketing the coin cheerfully. "I bet I can find all the others, too."

He started down the tunnel, staring intently at the ground.

"Rolly," Poppy said, "you do know that you don't get to keep the coins, right? You do remember that they belong to Dad—"

"Shh." Will elbowed her. "Don't distract him, not now when his criminal nature is finally coming in handy."

Poppy opened her mouth to argue, but then she saw Rolly square his shoulders, fix his eyes on something a few yards away, and start toward it with the single-minded focus of a hunting dog that has picked up a scent. If she had been standing a little closer to him, Poppy was sure she would have seen his nose twitch.

Seconds later, he snatched up another coin, put it in his pocket, and continued down the tunnel.

"You're right," said Poppy. "Anyway, I don't think we could stop him if we wanted to."

They pelted after Rolly through the dark tunnels, Poppy's flashlight illuminating their way with a thin and wavering beam of light. Rolly quickly found another coin, half hidden behind a boulder, but then he seemed to lose the trail, and for fifteen minutes, he wandered back and forth with Poppy, Will, and Franny following anxiously behind.

Just as Poppy was about to say they needed to

stop and come up with another plan, Rolly darted forward and ran down the dark and narrow tunnel that veered off to the left.

He skidded to a halt in front of a goblin door and bent down to pick up a coin, which had rolled to a stop just under another carving. This one had his lips pursed, as if he'd been caught in the act of spitting. Poppy had just noticed that the ground below the carving was more muddy than the rest of the tunnel floor when she saw Will step forward to take the coin from Rolly. . . .

And when he did, the goblin spat. A stream of water hit Will right in the face.

The cave erupted with laughter as Will spluttered and jumped back, landing heavily on Poppy's foot and pushing her off balance. She windmilled her arms, felt herself falling and, a few seconds later, sat down with a squelch in oozing mud.

"Ow!" Tears pricked her eyes. "That hurt."

Will wiped a sleeve across his face, then glared at her. "I didn't do it on purpose," he snapped.

"I didn't say you did," she snapped back.

"What are you two arguing about now?" asked Franny. She looked first at Will, wiping water off his face, then at Poppy, sitting in a mud puddle. "There's another coin right there in front of you."

Rolly's head swiveled around. "Where?"

He brightened as Franny pointed at a glint of gold on the ground. "I've got it!" he said, running over to snatch it up.

"Great, that's the last one," Will said. "Now all we have to do is find one of those trail signs Poppy made with the tape and Popsicle sticks, follow them back to where we started, climb out of the cave somehow—"

"Wait," Poppy said, but he wasn't listening.

She distinctly remembered dropping each coin along the side of the trail, hoping that Glitch wouldn't notice what she was doing. And yet the coin that Franny had found was lying smack-dab in the middle of the tunnel, right where anyone could see it. . . .

"Rolly! No, don't touch it," she cried, running toward the others.

But her warning came too late.

A net came down over Will, Franny, Rolly, and Poppy, tangling them in a web of ropes.

"All right, that's it, I've *had* it!" Poppy's voice rang through the rocky cavern.

Stupid, stupid, stupid, she thought. I knew that I hadn't dropped any coins in the middle of the tunnel, I knew that this was a trap. . . .

She grabbed the bottom of the net. "Come on. Let's get out of here."

Will and Franny followed her lead, but the result of three people attempting to lift a heavy net over their heads was not a happy one. Franny tried to duck under the net just as Will was lifting another section. He staggered back and pushed Poppy over. She grabbed a section of net to break her fall, which then twisted a rope around Franny, who landed with a grunt on Rolly.

And all the time they were struggling to escape, the sound of mocking goblin laughter was reverberating through the cave.

Finally, after stern instructions from Poppy, they managed to crawl out into the open air.

"Okay," said Will. "We're out. Now let's go—"

But when they turned to run, they found a familiar figure blocking their path.

"Nice try," said Glitch. He rubbed his hands together, grinning. "I love it when mortals think I've forgotten to lock the door. Or when they imagine they're being so clever by leaving a trail so they can find their way out."

His smile disappeared. "Did you really think we've lived in these caves for centuries without learning a few tricks of our own? Did you really think you'd come up with an escape plan that no one else has ever thought of? Did you really think we wouldn't notice you dropping gold coins behind you like bread crumbs?"

He shook his head, as if saddened by their utter lack of imagination. "All we had to do was pick them up and lay a trail of our own and . . . voila! We led you right back to where you started from."

Glitch crossed his arms over his chest and gave Poppy a particularly wide grin, as if he wanted to show as many of his sharp, pointed teeth as possible. "Face it," he continued. "You'll never find your way out of here."

Poppy took a deep breath. She grabbed Franny's hand with her right and Rolly's hand with her left, then locked eyes with Will.

"That's what you think," she said. Then she yelled one word.

"Run!"

They ran.

"You'll just get lost," Glitch called after them. "Hey! Look! We're not even bothering to chase you! Don't worry, when you get tired of trying to escape, we'll come get you. . . ."

His voice faded as they raced through dark tunnels, with Poppy trying to remember the twists and turns they'd taken, but mainly running as fast as she could to get away from the goblins.

And then they rounded a corner and stopped.

Poppy's heart sank as she realized where they were.

Dozens of candles flickered along the walls. Oil lamps burned with a warm, steady light, while cages of fireflies swung gently from wooden poles.

"We're back in Goblin Hall," Will said, disgusted. "We just came full circle."

Franny started to cry. "This is so unfair," she wept. "I haven't even turned sixteen yet! I haven't even lived! And now"—she pushed her hair back from her tear-stained face—"now I'm going to die in this stupid, stupid goblin cave!"

"No one's going to die," Poppy said testily. "There's got to be a way out of here."

"Oh, really?" Franny sounded dangerously close to hysteria. "Then where is it, Poppy? The goblins have moved all the coins you dropped, we can't find the trail markers you left behind, and no one knows we're here, thanks to you! If you think you can see a way out, I'd like to hear what it is—"

"Shh." Poppy held up one hand. She was thinking hard. They were in dire straits, no doubt about it. But she could feel the solution close at hand, so close that she could almost touch it. . . .

Slowly, she turned in a circle, examining every inch of her surroundings. There was the door to the prison cell, with its heavy oak planks and iron latch. And there was the carving of a goblin, winking at her as if he were taunting her with something that he knew and she didn't. . . .

And just like that, Poppy knew the answer to the puzzle that had been eluding her.

"We're not going to let those goblins beat us," she said, her voice firm with resolve. "I know exactly how to get us out of here."

"First, we need to douse all the lights so the goblins can't see us," she said.

"How do you know that will work?" Will asked. "What if they can see in the dark?"

"If they had adapted to the dark, they wouldn't need candles," Poppy said briskly. "They'd be like those fish and worms that live in caves for so long that they don't even have eyes anymore—"

Franny shuddered. "Thank you, Poppy. I had almost forgotten about the blind worms. And now I can also imagine running into goblins with no eyes. I'm feeling better already."

Poppy ignored her. She stood with her hands on her hips, surveying the cavern. "Franny, help me turn down the oil lamps," she said. "Will, Rolly, we need to open all the firefly cages and all the doors. Hurry!"

She and Franny moved quickly from one lamp to the next, carefully turning down the wicks until the flames were snuffed out. Rolly raced around the room, releasing swarms of fireflies that flew around the room a few times, then spiraled up into the darkness above their heads. Will flung open one door after another.

As he came to the last one, Poppy said, "Wait a second."

She reached into her backpack and pulled out a rope and a pair of night-vision goggles. After making three knots in the rope, she tied it around her waist, then handed the end to Rolly.

"Hold on to the first knot, Rolly, and don't let go," she said. "Franny, grab the second one, and Will, you take the third."

Once she was satisfied that they all had a firm grasp on the rope, she lowered the goggles over her eyes and nodded to Will.

"Okay," she said. "Now—open the door."

Will did and a gust of wind swept through the room. The candles guttered for a moment, then went out.

"Perfect," Poppy said. She turned off her flashlight, and they were plunged into complete darkness.

"Tell me again," Franny asked, "why this is a good idea?"

"Shh." Poppy scanned the room. With her goggles on, she could see the boulders, the tunnel opening, and most importantly, the goblin carving on the wall. "Follow me."

The night-vision goggles made the cave glow with a strange green light. Poppy moved confidently

through the darkness, occasionally passing whispered instructions to Rolly, Franny, and Will about
stepping around a puddle or over a rock.

They walked for ten yards before coming to
a side tunnel. Behind her, Franny said, "This is
crazy! We're all turned around, we have no idea
which way to go, we're going to get totally lost—"

"Shh." Poppy carefully examined the stone
walls, then pointed. "This way."

"Um, Poppy?" Will's voice, low and worried,
echoed back to them. "I know you've got everything figured out and you have a plan and all that,
but . . . are you sure?"

Poppy grinned in the dark. "Yep," she said.
"I'm sure."

The tunnel they took slanted down. Poppy
could feel some tugging on the rope, as if someone
(she suspected Franny) was resisting the idea that
they would actually walk deeper into the cave.

But five minutes later, they reached another
branching. This time, there were three tunnel
openings. Poppy walked slowly from one to the

other, peering up at the rock and pulling a reluctant group of people behind her.

"There," she said, pointing to a carving high on the wall. "This way."

She headed down the tunnel without any hesitation, moving so surely that the others had no choice but to follow.

The longer they walked, the more Will and Franny murmured darkly to themselves, but Poppy chose to ignore them. They came to five more intersections and were faced with five more choices. At each one, she paused just long enough to find the sign she was seeking before going on.

Finally, however, Will had had enough. He stopped dead and pulled on the rope to make everyone else stop, too.

"Hold on," he said. "Poppy, what are you doing? We've been walking for hours—"

Poppy glanced at her watch. "Actually, it's been fifteen minutes—"

"And the rest of us can't see a thing—"

"But I can," she said. "Trust me."

Even in the dark, Poppy could sense that Will was scowling at her.

"Do you have any idea where we are?" he demanded.

"Actually, I do." She turned on her flashlight and pointed it at the wall, where a goblin stuck out its tongue. "See that? Come on."

She pulled them after her as she rounded a corner and entered a small stone chamber. Weak morning light was filtering through a hole in the earth above them. Will and Franny blinked as Poppy grinned at them triumphantly.

"Here we are," she said. "Right back where we started from."

Once she knew the goblins' secret, Poppy explained to them all later, it was easy to find their way out of the cave.

"I couldn't figure out how the goblins were able to sneak around without us seeing them," she said. "And I knew they must have developed some kind of system to find their way through all the tunnels without getting lost themselves. When we ended up back in the cavern, I remembered that Muddle had entered through that one door—"

"The one with the goblin sticking his tongue out," Will said.

"Right," she said. "That was the sign showing the way out. All we had to do was follow it."

The four of them were walking through the woods toward home. When they'd gotten back to the cave entrance, Franny had hoisted Will up without any argument, and he had tied Poppy's rope to a tree. The others had pulled themselves up hand over hand, with Rolly clambering up first and Franny emerging last.

As they paused to catch their breaths, they looked at one another. Leaves and twigs were clinging to Franny's matted hair, Rolly had managed to tear a sleeve off his shirt, Will had brand-new scrapes and bruises on his legs, and Poppy was covered with dirt.

And yet, none of them could remember feeling happier.

They stepped out of the woods and looked at their house. It looked quiet and peaceful in the soft light of dawn. Birds chirped sleepily in the branches over their heads. A gentle breeze wafted by, carrying the sweet scents of cut grass and honeysuckle.

They heard a crash, followed by the faint sound of yelling. The kitchen window was flung open and a bundle of garlic was thrown, with some vehemence, onto the lawn.

Poppy smiled. It was good to be home.

EPILOGUE

"You're all up early," Mrs. Malone said as her children walked into the kitchen. She was sitting at the breakfast table with Mr. Malone and Oliver Asquith. They looked bleary eyed.

"Um, yeah," Will said. "You see—"

"We thought it might be fun to see the sun rise," said Poppy as Rolly climbed up on a chair.

Mr. Malone rubbed his hand over his face. "And was it?" He yawned.

She stared at him blankly. "What?"

He lowered his hand and glared at her. "Was it fun?"

"Oh yes! Yes!" Poppy said brightly. "In fact, it was so much fun, we think we might do it every morning."

Franny looked appalled, and Will kicked Poppy's ankle in protest.

"I keep telling you children that getting plenty of sleep is good for you." Yawning, Mrs. Malone stood up and began rooting through the cupboards. "I'm glad that you all managed to sleep through that little rumpus last night. . . ."

Franny perked up. "What kind of rumpus?"

"Can we have pancakes?" Rolly asked, reaching for the jar of honey in the center of the table.

"I think we'll just have cereal, dear heart," Mrs. Malone said over her shoulder. "I don't think I'm quite up to pancakes this morning."

"Were there vampires?" Franny persisted. Her face clouded over. "Please don't tell me that I missed meeting a real, live vampire—"

"Technically, vampires are dead," said her father, "and you'll be glad to know that you missed absolutely nothing except a bloodthirsty band of raccoons— Rolly, what are you *doing*?"

"What?" Rolly looked up innocently, seemingly unaware of the honey that was now dripping off the edge of the table. "Nothing."

Mr. Malone picked up a napkin and, with an irritable flourish, began dabbing at his knee. "Of course not," he muttered. "First raccoons, now this. What else can this day possibly bring—"

"You may well ask," Oliver Asquith said with a faint echo of his usual bravado. "I still say that those were no normal raccoons. They broke into the house! And did you see the way their eyes glowed with that unearthly red light?"

"What are you saying?" Mr. Malone scoffed. "That we fought off vampire raccoons?"

Oliver Asquith hesitated only a moment. "It's possible," he said. "More than possible, in fact—"

"Nonsense!" said Mr. Malone. "There's nothing remotely like that in any of the scientific literature."

Oliver Asquith sniffed. "Clearly, you haven't read my article in last month's issue of *Sanguinary Studies*," he said.

"Actually, I did," Mr. Malone said, his voice rising. "I found the premise faulty and the conclusions ridiculous."

"Really?" Oliver Asquith flung his head back, prepared to do battle. "Perhaps you'd like to defend that statement—"

"Dear, please." Mrs. Malone was pouring cereal with one hand and reaching for the aspirin bottle with the other. "I wonder if you two could continue your discussion elsewhere? It's most interesting, of course, but perhaps a bit *loud* for this early in the morning. . . ."

As Mr. Malone and Oliver Asquith disappeared into Mr. Malone's study, muttering to each other, Poppy slipped out of the kitchen and climbed the stairs to her room, eager to record all that had happened in her logbook.

First, though, she opened the door to Rolly's bedroom and peeked inside.

The bed was neatly made. The toys were in the toy chest, the clothes picked up off the floor. Other than that, there was no sign that a goblin child had ever lived there.

Poppy was surprised to realize that she would, in some way, miss the changeling. He could never replace Rolly, of course, but he had been rather sweet, not to mention quiet, polite, and remarkably tidy. Not really very goblinlike at all, really. . . .

Then she spotted the tiny footprints on the floor. There were two sets—apparently made with red paint. The footprints circled the bed, splotched a chair cushion, smeared the windowsill, and then ran across the porch roof.

Poppy sighed. She would have to clean this mess up before anyone else saw it. Vampires were bad enough, but she shuddered at the thought of her parents' reaction if they realized they could investigate actual goblins. And as for Oliver Asquith! They'd never get rid of him if he got wind of this—

"Oh no!"

Poppy jumped at the sound of her mother's voice, then turned to see Mrs. Malone and Rolly standing in the hall behind her.

"Honestly, Rolly, this is the last straw!" said Mrs. Malone, glaring at the footprints marching jauntily across the room. "I haven't had a wink of sleep, I've spent hours listening to your father and Oliver arguing about the silliest things, and I absolutely reek of garlic. And now this! Rolly, what were you *thinking*?"

Rolly's black eyebrows drew together. His lower lip jutted out. "But I didn't—"

"Do it," snapped Mrs. Malone. "Of course you didn't. You never do *anything*, Rolly, and yet disaster seems to follow you wherever you go—"

"But I wasn't me! It was Glitch!" Rolly's face darkened. "And that *Blot*!"

His mother wasn't listening. She had walked over to the bed, where she stood staring bleakly at the floor. "That rug will probably have to be dry cleaned. I'm sorry, but this time I think you need a time out."

Rolly's face looked even stormier.

"But I wasn't even HERE!" he yelled. "I was in a CAVE! With GOB—"

"Please don't shout, dear," Mrs. Malone said, pressing a hand to her forehead. "The aspirin hasn't started working yet. Now I'm going downstairs to get some cleaning supplies. I suggest you sit quietly on your bed—quietly, Rolly!—and think about what you've done."

As Mrs. Malone headed toward the door, Poppy saw Rolly climb onto his bed and stand there, his hands on his hips, his dark eyes snapping with fury. "This is not my fault!" he cried. "I keep trying to tell you about the weird stuff happening in this house and you won't even listen to me!"

Mrs. Malone stopped midstride and stood absolutely still. Her eyes met Poppy's. "Of course!" she whispered. "I should have thought of this in the first place. Small children are extraordinarily sensitive to otherworldly vibrations."

She turned around slowly, as if trying not to startle Rolly, and peered intently into his small, fierce eyes. "I'm listening now, Rolly," she said in a low, soothing voice. "Tell me exactly what you saw."

Rolly smirked triumphantly and opened his mouth to answer. For a fleeting moment, Poppy thought of diving across the room and tackling him, but she immediately dismissed the idea as ridiculous. The bed was too far away. Rolly was too experienced at avoiding body tackles. And it was too late, anyway. The secret was out. . . .

"I saw a goblin," Rolly began. "His name is Glitch. He's little and has beady eyes and lots of pointy teeth—"

"I knew it!" Mrs. Malone exclaimed with delight. "I knew I was right!"

Poppy's heart sank. "We shouldn't jump to conclusions," she said weakly. "Maybe Rolly just saw a shadow or something and imagined that it was a goblin—"

"I can't wait to tell your father," her mother went on, ignoring her. "I *knew* there was a Dark Presence in this house!"

Poppy's mouth dropped open. She glanced at Rolly, who looked as baffled as she felt. "But Rolly said—"

"That he saw a goblin, I know," said Mrs. Malone with a wave of her hand. "But clearly, what he *actually* saw was an unhappy spirit that chose to appear to him in a way that he would understand.

And young children are most familiar with fairy tales, which, of course, are often populated with goblins." Her eyes were bright with excitement. "Oh, this is wonderful news!"

She hugged Rolly and even kissed him on the forehead before he managed to squirm free. "No time out, my dear. Now I must go and tell your father—he will be so pleased!"

She rushed out of the room and was gone.

Rolly dropped to his knees, bounced once on the bed, then flung himself back on the mattress. "It's not fair," he said to the ceiling. "No one *ever* believes me. No one *ever* listens to me. And when anything goes wrong, everyone always says it's *my* fault."

"Look on the bright side," Poppy said, yawning. "From now on, you can always just blame the Dark Presence."

"Mm." Rolly gave this a few seconds of serious consideration before the corner of his mouth lifted in a tiny smile. "That's actually a very good idea, Poppy. Thank you."

For a moment, he sounded so much like Blot

that Poppy felt a shiver of unease. "Um, well, you're welcome, Rolly, but I wasn't *serious* about that—"

He turned his head far enough to give her the blank stare that meant that his mind was far away, busily concocting some new plot. "Oh, that's okay," he said vaguely. "I was."

Poppy saw the corner of his mouth lift in a tiny smile. She hesitated, wondering if she should ask what, exactly, he was planning to pin on the Dark Presence . . . then decided that she was too tired.

I'll wait to find out with the rest of the family, she thought, blinking sleepily as she headed down the hall to her bedroom. I just hope this time there won't be sirens.

When Poppy opened her door, she stared longingly at her bed. It looked so inviting, with its fluffy pillows and comfortable quilt and soft mattress. . . .

Then she blinked several times, opened her eyes extra-wide, and pinched herself for good measure before sitting cross-legged on the hard wooden floor.

The only way to maintain a clear and accurate scientific record, she reminded herself firmly, was to take notes while one's observations were still fresh.

She flipped open her notebook. There would be plenty of time for sleeping later.

She pulled a pencil out of her pocket. I'll just jot down a few notes to get my thoughts on paper. Then I'll let myself take a nice, long nap. . . .

Ten minutes later, Poppy was still staring at the blank page, chewing on the end of her pencil, and wondering where to begin.

The problem wasn't being tired or sleepy. The problem was much simpler than that: She was afraid. Afraid that if she wrote it all down—that she had seen goblins, talked to them, outwitted them, even—if she put it on paper, people might find out. Then she'd never fit in, never have friends, never be normal. . . .

Maybe I've inherited some kind of weird gene from Mom and Dad, she thought gloomily. Maybe I'm doomed to spend my life searching for UFOs and lake monsters and things that go bump in the night.

She slapped the notebook closed. *No*, she thought. Moving hundreds of miles to a new town had given her a chance to start over, and she planned to make the most of it.

I'll just keep quiet, she thought. No one has to know about the goblins. No one has to know anything.

But almost as soon as the idea came to her, she dismissed it, a brief feeling of giddy relief vanishing like snow in August.

For better or worse, Poppy was a scientist. She had to write the truth, even if it meant that people laughed at her. Even if it meant she was unpopular. Even if—

I will record everything that happened, she thought, because that's what a true scientist would do. I'll just make sure that no one ever reads it.

Carefully, Poppy wrote a warning on the notebook cover. She made each letter big and bold, then darkened it with her pencil to make sure there was no doubt about what it said.

"Do not open for one hundred years," she wrote.

"At that time, the contents may be published, if it is deemed by the authorities that they will not lead to mass hysteria and public unrest. Until then, the knowledge contained in this book must remain Top Secret and Classified."

She read that over a few times to make sure it struck the right note of danger. Then, with a flourish, she added one more line:

"By Order of the Author, Poppy Malone."

Satisfied, she opened the notebook and began writing.

"I'm not the kind of girl who sees goblins," she wrote. "If it had been anyone else in my family, it would have made a lot more sense. But they didn't go into the attic on that hot June afternoon. I did, and that made all the difference. . . ."